THE BROKEN
AND
THE BRAVE

THE DRAGON QUEEN #1.5

EC GARRETT

Collector's Edition Cover Illustration by Reina Diaz

Interior Formatting and Design by EC Garrett

Special Edition Hardcover Illustrations by Reina Diaz

Interior Illustrations by Reina Diaz

Line-Item Editing and Proofreading by YarnWyvern

eBook ISBN: 979-8-9890690-9-5

Paperback ISBN: 978-1-965919-00-2

Collector's Edition Hardback

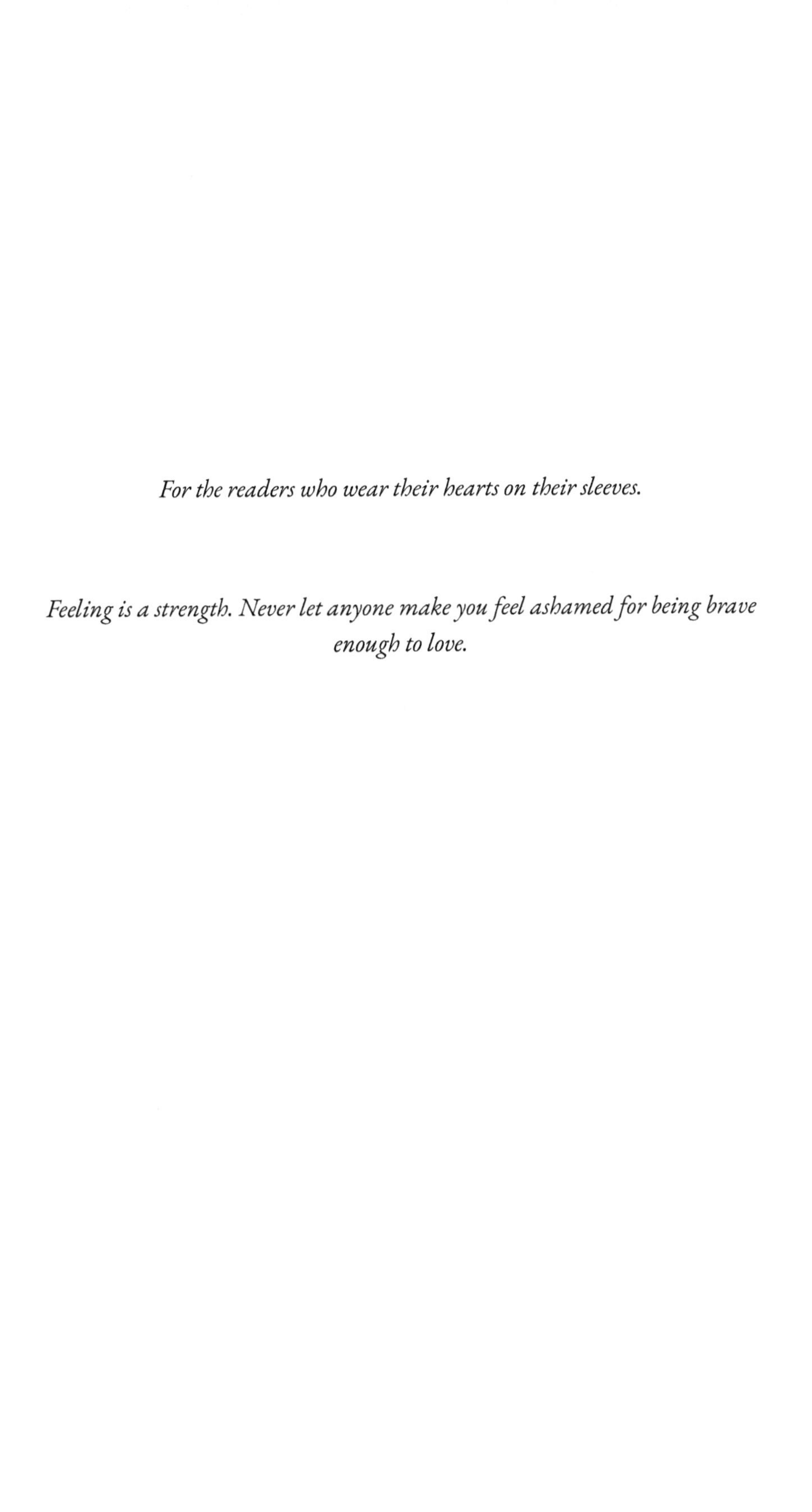

For the readers who wear their hearts on their sleeves.

Feeling is a strength. Never let anyone make you feel ashamed for being brave enough to love.

THE DRAGON QUEEN

SERIES READING ORDER

The Forgotten and The Feared

The Broken and The Brave

The Defiant and The Damned – 2/25/25

A NOTE FROM THE AUTHOR

The Broken and The Brave is a companion novel to **The Forgotten and The Feared.** While not required to read the series, it provides key insight and alternative perspectives from the characters you've come to know and love. It might also contain some major hints of what's to come...Enjoy!

The Broken and The Brave is divided into **three parts:**

PART ONE: THE BEFORE

Takes place before the events of The Forgotten and The Feared

PART TWO: THE BRAVE

Takes place during The Forgotten and The Feared.

PART THREE: THE BROKEN

Takes place during the two-year time jump at the end of The Forgotten and The Feared, bridging the gap between it and The Dragon Queen: Book #2, The Defiant and The Damned. **The Broken and The Brave** is a companion novel to **The Forgotten and The Feared**. While not required to read the series, it provides key insight and alternative perspectives from the character

TWYN FELLS
THE ULSTER WALD
THE PASS OF BRÓN MÓR
NORTHLANDS
ABHYANN GHEAL RIVER
EAHMOND
WESTLANDS
INFINIUM SANDS
SOUTHLANDS

THE KINGDOM OF UR DAOINE
CASTAEL LARYN
MIDHEYM SEA
EASTLANDS
SUD AZYL

A WARNING:

The Dragon Queen series is set in a Grimdark, medieval fantasy world, with a high amount of violence, gore, and danger. All incidents involving animals are inspired by the real life cruelty animals in our world experience every second of every day. If The Dragon Queen series was a movie, it would be rated R or NC-17 due to graphic violence, graphic sex, language, and dire situations. Proceed with caution and review the trigger warning list below before you dive in. If it all sounds good? Then **let the Game begin.**

Triggers that are frequent are in **BOLD** and triggers that are extremely frequent are in **<u>BOLD AND UNDERLINED.</u>**

HATE, DISCRIMINATION, & OPPRESSION

Bullying, Classism, Disownment, Gentrification, Hate Crimes, Homelessness, Lesbomisia, Queermisia, **<u>Poverty</u>**, Racism, **<u>Religious Persecution, Religious Commentary,</u> Sexism & Misogyny**, Slavery & Indentured Servitude, and Slut-Shaming

SEXUAL & ROMANTIC

<u>Age Gap</u>, **Fingering**, **Masturbation**, M/M, M/F, Unrequited Love.

MENTAL HEALTH & SUICIDE

Anxiety & Anxiety Attacks, Depression, Dissociation & Dissociative Episodes, Intrusive thoughts, **Nightmares, <u>Post Traumatic Stress Disorder,</u>** Self-harm, Sleep Disorders, and **Suicidal Ideation.**

INJURY & MEDICAL

Amputation, **<u>Blood & Gore Depiction,</u>** Body Horror, **<u>Dead Bodies & Body Parts,</u> Decapitation, Dismemberment,** Emesis, **Eyeball Trauma, Loss of Autonomy, <u>Physical Injuries,</u> Scars,** Starvation & Dehydration, Weight Gain

DEATH & LOSS

Death of a child, Death of a friend, <u>Death of a Parent & Guardian,</u> Death of a Partner & Spouse, **Death of a Sibling, <u>Grief & Loss Depiction</u>**

VIOLENCE & CRIME

Asphyxia, Strangulation & Suffocation, **Blackmail, <u>Building Collapse,</u> Captivity & confinement, <u>Cults,</u>** Explosions, **<u>Fire & Arson</u>**, Imprisonment & Incarceration, **<u>Knife, sword & axe violence, Murder & attempted murder,</u>** Physical assault, Stalking, and **<u>Whipping</u>**

WAR & GENOCIDE

<u>Colonialism, Imperialism,</u> Massacres & mass murder, and War themes & military violence

ANIMAL DEATH & CRUELTY

Animal Attack, **Animal Consumption, <u>Animal Cruelty & Abuse, Animal Death, Animal Illness & Injury, Animal Skinning/Butchering,</u>** Animal Testing & Experimentation, Forced Breeding, and Hunting.

THE LANGUAGE

CHARACTERS

Amalia: *uh-MAH-lee-uh*

Achan: *AH-kin*

Aanad: *uh-NOD*

Constantus: *con-STAN-tus*

Constantyn: *con-STAN-teen*

Drayven: *Dray-ven*

Dyana: *die-AN-uh*

Embyrne: *EM-burn*

Ireyna: *eye-REY-nuh*

Kydis: *KAI-diss*

Landys: *LAN-diss*

Larousse: *LUH-roos*

Mireille: *MEER-ee-el*

Morrigyn: *MORE-ih-ghin*

Nyall: *NY-uhl*

Os: *oz*

Remus: *REE-mus*

Ryu: *REE-you*

Syska: *SIS-kuh*

Vesimyr: *VES-uh-meer*

PLACES

Abhaynn Gheal: *ah-VEEN geel*

Annag: *AHH-nug*

Brón Mór: *BRON more*

Castael Laryn: *KAY-stil LAIR-in*

Elysium: *uh-LEE-see-um*

Infinium: *in-FIN-ee-um*

Livyathin: *luh-VIE-uh-thin*

Midheym: *MID-high-m*

Österhamn: *OO-ster-hahm*

Sud Azyl: *sood a-ZEAL*

Twyn Fells: *twin fells*

Ulster Wald: *UHL-ster vahld*

Ur Daoine: *ur DANE-ya*

<u>OTHER TERMS</u>

A gahrá: *ah GAH-ruh*

Ahavah: *uh-HAH-vah*

Alle Seele: *ALL-uh SELL-uh*

Arkaydian: *are-KAY-dee-in*

Arkaydia: *are-KAY-dee-uh*

Beastkyn: *BEAST-kin*

Ether: *EE-thur*

Demis: *DEM-ees*

Lir: *leer*

Lesbos: *LESS-bahs*

Macha: *MAH-kuh*

Magyka: *MA-jik-uh*

Magyk: *MA-jik*

Neiman: *NEE-man*

Oryx: *OR-icks*

Puggō: *POO-gogh*

Wytch: *wich*

THE BROKEN
AND
THE BRAVE

SCAN FOR THE OFFICIAL
READING PLAYLIST

PROLOGUE

I do not remember my mother—she died after giving birth to me.

She survived the birth itself, but after she made sure I was alive and healthy, my mother stabbed a knife into her own heart, refusing to sire another half-breed Elf.

Death was a better alternative than my father.

Achan Drayven; High Councilor of Ur Daoine and my sire.

Ur Daoine means "New Fae" in our language. My first memory is my father trying to teach me to pronounce it. I blundered the words, as most children would, so Achan beat me with his belt, my cries falling on unhearing ears.

That became our pattern.

Please him...or feel the pain of resistance.

Children are so easy to manipulate. I didn't always hate him. I *idolized* him. If only I had learned the truth. If only I had seen who he really was.

By the time I finally saw the truth...it was too late.

My name is Nyall Drayven, and this is my story.

"I MADE MY OWN
HOUSE BE MY GALLOWS."

— DANTE ALIGHIERI, 1265–1321.
THE DIVINE COMEDY: INFERNO

PART ONE:
THE BEFORE

CHAPTER 1
NYALL

14 years after the end of the Great War (Year 14 PBM)

The Dragon Pit stinks of blood, urine, and feces mixed with steaming sulfur. The humidity in the air makes it all the more pungent.

I hold back a gag. Though I'm 30 years old, I'm still considered a child in the eyes of the High Council. Untested and untrained—which is why I'm down here. As *punishment.*

Father said I must see the beasts and work in the stables for a month.

"You're too soft, *boy.* You need to see the evil bastards up close. Then you'll understand. They do not belong in the wild, they belong here where we can *control* them!" Father shook my shoulders, shouting in my face. "They are a power to be claimed."

He's always said this; always *hated* the Dragons. As the years have passed, it's bothered me more and more.

But when I am with him, I still feel like a child. Afraid to speak up for myself and voice my opinions.

I know what he does to those who disagree with him, who challenge him. Violence is how my father solves *everything.*

I scoop the piles of Dragon shit out of the empty stall, wincing under the weight of it. The rake nearly breaks beneath the large pile as I lift and dump it into the wheelbarrow to my left. I don't know where they take the Dragons when they leave here, and I'm not sure I want to ask.

Something clatters in the distance, and I freeze. The noise echoes through the big chamber. Another clatter sounds, like something banging into a metal wall.

Something *big*.

Don't be soft. The Pit is full of Dragons. That's all you heard. A Dragon dragging their claw against their stall.

Sometimes, the voice in my head sounds so much like my father.

The rest of the guards leave.

There are overnight guards, but they stay at the top of the Pit. Most of them live on the upper floors, which are made up of small dormitories to house our armies and workers.

That's what Father claimed, at least. There have always been *whispers* about his cruelty. Everyone has *always* feared Achan Drayven. But in the past two years, that fear has tasted especially sharp.

After the High Council destroyed Morrigyn's temple, the first thing they did was empty the pit and begin building the stalls. The Archmage placed warding spells on every stall door, ensuring the Dragons couldn't use their magyk to open it.

Father declared that I would work the overnight shift. It's the least desirable time to be stuck hundreds of meters underground. There's no light down here, so I easily lose track of time.

Another clatter and I drop the rake, startled out of my own thoughts.

That didn't sound like it came from any stall.

The noise repeats, only this time, it's farther away. The sound echoes through-out the large cavern, magnifying it.

What the hell is down here? Curiosity begs me to investigate, but I know what happens to those who get curious.

They get *punished.*

"Soft." I hear my father's voice again in my thoughts. He said it with such disgust. As if my empathy and kindness was a contagious sickness.

A thread of anger weaves around my heart, making me burn with resentment.

I am not *soft*. Leaving my rake and wheelbarrow in the vacant stall, I follow the sound around the corner, out into the hallway between two rows of stables.

High-pitched whines come out of the occupied stalls. Huge, glowing eyes watch me. They throw their bodies against the cage door, roaring in pain.

The doors don't budge.

I try not to look into their eyes. Try not to look at them at all. A part of me is afraid of what will happen if I do.

Trailing through the rows of stables, I keep following the clattering until I'm in the deepest, darkest corner of the Pit. The stables end and it's just tunnels of damp rock. Darkness descends as I keep going, following the noise.

Light shines ahead, but it's faint. I turn another corner and find a metal ramp.

Metal...that means the Fae built this. But there's no light.

Are they hiding something?

My boots slide around the slick floor as I make my way up the ramp. At the top, I come to a stop as my jaw hits the floor.

A sort of nesting area, full of shavings, is surrounded by gates.

The gate isn't shocking.

The Dragon Eggs arranged in a tight circle is.

Multi-colored in rich jewel tones, the thick eggs sit on the shavings, closely packed together. But one of the eggs—it's *moving*. The eggs are *hatching*. I didn't even know we had Dragon Eggs, let alone what to do if one hatches.

Does my father know about this? Do they know the eggs are here?

Thoughts racing, I walk over to the edge of the gate, getting a closer look at the hatching egg.

My hands have barely touched the cold metal when a low, hissing sound sets my hair on end.

I drop my hands as if the metal shocked me. The sound stops.

Huh.

The Dragons cannot escape, thanks to the Archmage's ward. Surely that sound came from the stables behind me.

The cavern must be making the sound seem closer.

Yes. That's all it was.

I place my hands back on the gate and crouch down, looking at the egg. It cracks again and I hear a tiny, muffled squeak come from inside of it.

Hissssssssssssssssss. The sound is louder this time. So loud, it vibrates the metal beneath my palms. I drop my hands again, but the sound doesn't stop.

No, it gets louder. Dust begins to fall from the ceiling and the walls groan.

My heart stops and I let my senses take over.

Something *is* here. Something else.

It hides, but I can feel its presence and sense its eyes watching me.

The shavings rumble, shifting just slightly and I nearly fall backwards.

It's beneath the shavings. Beneath the eggs.

What are you?

The hissing sound deepens, turning into a growl that rattles my bones. My heart races.

"So fucking soft. Just like your Mother. Soft and weak."

Father's voice echoes in my thoughts.

~~*WHY IS IT SO BAD IF I'M LIKE HER?*~~

No! I am not weak!

I stop backing up and lift my chin.

I am no child. If the creature wants a fight, I'll give it one. This is *my* domain. My *kingdom.*

The Dragon Egg cracks some more as part of the shell falls off and a small blue head poke out. The shavings in the hatching area *move* as the creature emerges.

My jaw drops and I watch in equal parts awe and terror as a huge black Dragon rises from beneath the egg. It crawls around the hatchling, protecting it.

Adrenaline shoots through my body.

Dragonfear, they call it.

A primal reaction to witnessing the true apex predator of this world. I swallow it, suffocating the fear the way I suffocate the pain doled out at my father's hands.

The Dragon watches me, baring huge, ivory fangs and black gums. Eyes of pure, burning gold watch me carefully. Its onyx scales are covered in scars, but they don't take away from the magnificence. Black horns decorate the Dragon's head.

It flares its black nostrils, sending a wave of smoke at my face. I hold my breath as it blows past me.

Father said when Dragons reach one year old, they begin rapidly maturing, growing nearly full size by age two. They continue to mature, growing bigger and bigger, over thousands and thousands of years.

This one could be easily be a thousand years old.

I back away slowly, not wanting to disturb it anymore. As soon as the Dragon sees that I'm leaving, it calms. Maybe it's the mother of the eggs, then. Its golden eyes never leave me. I can *feel* it watching, tracing my every step. Goosebumps decorate my arms.

Wait.

The realization hits me.

The Dragon...how did it get in here? How is it out of its stall?

CHAPTER 2
OS

I do not enjoy the taste of Fae flesh. It has a bitter aftertaste, the meat lean and tough.

I prefer animals that are plump and sweet. Lambs, goats, and occasionally large birds of prey.

As I look at the young Fae male before me, I reconsider my precious stance.

My mouth begins to salivate; it's been weeks since I left the hatchlings, since I last fed. Dragons can go up to a month without eating, but weakness has begun to creep in. I can feel it.

I didn't feel safe leaving them alone. Not here.

Not with *them* nearby.

The Fae male appears young. His flesh might be sweeter. The male's body appears to be that of someone in their mid-twenties—but there is a naivety about his movements.

Not a child, but not an adult.

The young Fae isn't a soldier, either. Not yet at least. Sweat and dirt stain his finely made clothes. It's not his appearance that makes me pause.

No. It's the look in his eyes. It's the air of authority in his movements. A certain confidence reserved for those with power.

He's an Imperial Fae.

My mouth dries up.

No, his flesh will not be sweet. He's rotten to the core like the rest of them. Imperial Fae cunts.

The Fae's little heart races and the air turns thick with the scent of his fear.

Good. I feed on your fear, little Fae. Be afraid, for I will tear you limb from limb.

The egg beneath me cracks again, and a loud squeak follows. I'm yanked out of my thoughts. I glance down as the hatchling pushes through the top of its shell.

The inside of the egg is dark, but I can see bright green eyes next to dark, navy scales still gleaming with amniotic fluid.

A baby blue.

The hatchling trills, looking for its mother. It finds me instead, locking eyes with me. It squeaks louder and wiggles around, trying to break open the rest of its shell. A small, delicate snout emerges.

Hatchlings always remind me of my sister. I miss her so much it makes my heart ache, but the knowledge that she's safe back in Elysium keeps me going.

She is safe.

She's *free.* That's all that matters.

The hatchling pushes through more of the eggshell, the broken shards falling into the soft shavings. The egg is open enough that the hatchling tumbles out. It wavers, unable to stand.

Round green eyes watch me.

"Mama?" a small voice asks in my head.

"No," I reply softly. *"I am not mama. I am a friend. But I will look after you."*

"Friend!" it squeaks happily. The hatchling attempts to roll over, but it falls face first into the shavings.

I right the little one, tucking its delicate wings in so that they won't get torn. I pull the hatchling tight against my chest, letting it feel the fire burning in my belly.

Hatchlings love warmth, so the baby blue goes right to sleep. It will need to feed soon. But hatching takes a lot of energy. I'm not surprised the little one is tired.

I realize I've taken my eyes off the boy, but when I look up, the young Fae male is gone.

The second he's out of my sight, worry worms its way into my heart.

Fuck. I should have killed him! Because now...someone knows I'm here.

The moment my stall opened, unbidden and seemingly without reason, I knew it was a sign of bad tidings to come. I could have escaped. Could have crawled out of here, digging my way to the surface...

I thought about it, but...I can't leave the younglings.

CHAPTER 3
NYALL

I should tell Father. But for some reason...I don't.

I can't stop thinking about it, the Black Dragon and the hatchling.

I stood there, watching as the Dragon finally took its eyes off me. The way it cradled the hatchling to it, nuzzling it with so much love...more love than I have ever seen or felt in my life.

Father has always said that the Dragons are unfeeling, evil, killing machines.

But...that didn't seem evil.

It seemed *loving.* A seed of doubt settles into my thoughts. A seed of *uncertainty.*

If the Dragons aren't evil...then does that mean my father is?

"What the fuck am I doing?" I grumble, tracing the same path I took yesterday.

I barely slept a wink all day. The only thing I could think about was the Black Dragon and the hatchlings. Every time I closed my eyes, I saw golden eyes watching me.

I have three more weeks of Dragon Pit duty. Twenty-one nights of shoveling shit.

An idea occurs to me as I walk into the abandoned part of the Pit.

I've been studying under the Archmage for almost a decade.

If the Archmage laid warding onto the stall doors…maybe I could lay a ward in the corner?

A *shield* ward.

It's one of the first weavings I learned. The Archmage used it during the Great War to distract any enemies who approached the city.

I take a deep breath and lift my palms, summoning my magyk. Ropes of white light weave around my arms, signaling my power is awake.

Tracing the sigyl for 'Shield' in the air, I pull on my power and weave the spell together. It flashes in the air before raining down on the ground.

There's a sharp pain as it snaps into place.

Good.

I make it up that metal ramp and peek around the corner. Now that I know what to look for, I can see where the Dragon is hiding beneath the shavings. The hatchling is nowhere to be seen, just the broken pieces of eggshell.

There are four more Dragon Eggs, but I have no idea when they will hatch. Taking a deep breath, I step forward.

"I know you're here, Dragon. I mean no harm."

The Dragon does not respond.

"I am not here to hurt you or the eggs."

A loud hissing sound follows as the pile of shavings moves and the Black Dragon emerges, its golden eyes fierce. The Dragon continues to lift out of the shavings, hovering over me in a clear attempt at intimidation.

The Dragon doesn't realize that it need not try to intimidate me; the sheer size of it does that already.

Does it even understand me? Father says that part of why the Dragons are so evil is that they pray to some ancient, eldritch God named Livyathin.

Sol Constantus preaches that there is only one God, and His name is Constantyn.

There are no other Gods but *Him.*

"Livyathin is the truest evil," Father always said. "The Dragons sacrifice their young to him in exchange for power. They pledge their lives in blood to serve his will."

"What is Livyathin's will?" I asked. The first time I heard this story was when I was ten years old.

That's when Father deemed me old enough for the truth of the Great War and what happened.

"To take over this world. To enslave us to his will. That's why they must die, my son. All of the Dragons must die."

Now, as I stand here, I question the truth of my father's words. I've been doing a lot of that, lately.

Questioning him.

The hissing grows softer. Not going silent, but lessening. The Dragon still bares its teeth at me. It leans forward until its snout is so close, I could reach up and touch it.

God, it's huge.

The Dragon growls and my legs nearly give out, but I force the fear away. It will not be my master.

"I mean no harm," I say again, my voice no louder than a whisper. The Dragon leans to the side and lowers its head until we're eye to eye.

Its fangs are longer than my fucking legs.

This is it. The Dragon is going to eat me.

Then the growling stops and the Dragon withdraws, watching me carefully, its golden eyes missing nothing.

Maybe it does understand me.

"I just came here to say that if you stay in here, you won't be seen. I'm going to lay a spell on the entrance. It will encourage others to walk past and muffle some noise. Not all, but some."

The Dragon watches me carefully. There's a squeak as the blue hatchling emerges, its small head poking out of the shavings near the Black Dragon's leg.

The hatchling begins to cry, and I swear, both the Dragon and I jump slightly, unsure what to do. The young Dragon's cries are loud and agonized.

Fuck. My wards won't silence cries this loud. This isn't good.

The Dragon nuzzles the hatchling, trying to calm it, but it doesn't work. I glance behind me, worried the noise will alert the others.

My spell will detract attention, but it doesn't cover up much sound.

"I think...it's hungry," I suggest, as the hatching keeps crying.

The Dragon looks at me like I'm an idiot.

"Feed it," I try to mime the action and wince. "Uh, never mind. Sorry."

The Dragon sighs and rolls its eyes. The action is so human, I nearly stumble. Then the Dragon starts to glow.

One second the black Dragon is normal, the next, bright light shoots out from it. I'm forced to cover my eyes against the searing burn. Even then, it hurts my eyelids.

Everything goes black as the light disappears.

I carefully open my eyes, blinking against the colorful aftershock.

"I cannot *feed* it," a low voice says. "Nor is it my young."

The voice is *male.*

I backpedal, gasping as my vision clears and I take in the sight before me.

The Dragon is gone and in its place is a male. A male with eyes of burning gold. He towers over me; the tallest male I've ever seen. With wide, muscular shoulders and deep umber skin.

"You-you—" I stammer, my mind exploding.

The male scoffs, "Yes, yes. I am a Dragon. Now, I need your help. I need milk for the hatchlings, or they will die."

I blink rapidly, "Excuse me?"

"You heard me." The Dragon grabs the hatchling, holding it in his arms as he strides out of the shavings.

"Can't its mother nurse it?" I ask carefully.

The male snarls at me, his nails lengthening into black claws. "Your people *killed* their mother. They are orphans."

Guilt plagues me at his words.

"A victim of war, it seems," I clear my throat.

The male scoffs. "No. A victim of the Fae."

I look away, uncomfortable with his words, and even more uncomfortable with the truth within them.

"I need milk for them, boy."

"Boy?" I whip my head around and face him. "I'm no child—" my words cut off, fading away on the tip of my tongue as I take in the sight before me.

I was so shocked with the reality of his shifting that I hadn't fully realized…

The Dragon is *very* naked.

A warm, fuzzy feeling rushes through me at the sight of his thick cock dangling between his legs. He's stacked with thick layers of muscle. Every centimeter of the Dragon's form projects violence.

A soldier. A *fighter.*

"Where exactly do you suggest I find milk for the hatchlings? They don't exactly sell Dragon milk around here."

The Dragon hisses at me, the sound far less scary in this form. I wave him off and the Dragon blinks, surprised.

"Do you have farm animals here? Cows, goats, lambs?" the Dragon asks.

I nod, "Yeah, we do. There's a farm just outside the western part of the city.

"Good. That will suffice for the hatchlings."

I scratch my head. "Right then. How much milk do you need?"

What the fuck am I doing? Am I really going to do this? Steal from my own people to feed the young of our supposed enemy?

But they don't seem evil. What if they're not our enemies? ~~*What if Father is WRONG?*~~

"As much as you can bring," the Dragon responds, his voice tinged with desperation. "The other eggs will hatch soon; I can feel it. In a matter of days, there will be four more mouths to feed."

"I cannot hide you forever," I say carefully. "Eventually they will find you in here. You know that, right?"

His face turns furious instantly. The look in his eyes is so cutting, it almost hurts.

"You are a royal," he says, eyes narrowing. "Your scent...it is familiar."

I stiffen and nod, tightly.

How the hell did the Dragon figure that out?

"There is a reason Dragons were once revered as Gods, young Prince." The Dragon's voice is suddenly in my head, and I nearly jump out of my skin.

"Get out of my head," I growl.

He smirks, and it's a thing of beauty and violence. "You couldn't stop me even if you tried. But perhaps if you help me, I won't torment your every waking move."

Well, well. Dragons can be manipulative, then.

I've been pushed into a corner. Crossing my arms, I lift my chin. The Dragon is still taller than me in this form, but I can still meet his gaze.

"Your eyes," he whispers in my head. *"They are quite strange."*

I look away, embarrassed. A hand grabs my chin and turns my head, forcing me to look into his eyes.

"What is your name, Fae Prince?"

"Nyall," I answer aloud. "Nyall Drayven."

The Dragon drops my chin and steps back, growling.

"Drayven? Achan Drayven is your father?" His voice is so full of fury, I nearly fall to my knees.

I nod, "Yes."

"Then I pity you," The Dragon turns and walks back into the nursing area. With a bright flash of light, he returns to Dragon form, burrowing down until his scales disappear, covered by shavings and pieces of eggshells.

"What a terrible thing it must be, having that evil prick as a sire."

CHAPTER 4
OS

The Fae doesn't like when I admonish his father. He spouts off some nonsense about how his father isn't bad. Just...passionate.

I ignore him. There is no reason to respond, or to hear him out. He will not help me. He is Achan Drayven's child, after all.

The Fae who led the Great War. Whose actions slaughtered thousands, and who is the reason we're in this prison. This pit.

I tuck the blue hatchling close and curl my large body around it, trying to soothe it to sleep. My face ends up right next to it, and through the shadows and shavings, I watch it in awe.

"Friend," it murmurs sleepily. *"I hungry, friend."*

"I know," my voice is desperate, *"I'll find food for you tomorrow...somehow."*

The hatchling falls asleep, but I do not.

How can I, when I can hear the little one's stomach grumbling?

Eventually, the Prince falls silent, and I listen as his footsteps lead him away.

As I thought; all Fae are the same.

Something hard wakes me.

Hunger plagues me as well. They barely feed us down here.

I open my eyes and push out of the shavings to see a large bottle full of milk.

Looking up, I watch as the Prince throws another bottle at my feet. The bottle bounces off my claws.

He...he's helping me. Why?

"Goats milk. I hope that's enough." The Prince looks down at his hands, hesitating. "I thought you might be hungry as well..." The Fae Prince takes a deep breath and summons his magyk. Symbols made of white light show up on his hands and arms.

This magyk; it doesn't look Fae.

What are you hiding, Prince? What is this strange magyk you use?

The Prince makes a gesture with his hands, and a whole, dead pig falls at my feet.

I would ask where it came from, but right now, I don't care.

The hatchling beneath me squeaks and I put away my hunger. It needs to feed first. Grabbing a bottle with my claws, I put it to the hatchling's mouth. It takes a few moments for the hatchling to figure it out, but eventually, it pulls the rubber nipple between its still soft teeth and begins to drink.

I sigh in relief.

"Thank you," I whisper in the Prince's head.

His mind is poorly guarded. Connecting with him took only a thought. The Prince nods.

"Why did you help me?" I ask, genuinely curious.

Why would my enemy help me?

"We are not evil," the Prince says quietly, his eyes pure and earnest. "Not all of us, at least."

I blink.

"So, you admit, your father is evil."

"I—" the Prince takes a breath and looks away. "I do not think he is, but...I think there is much I still do not know."

This is someone who has been manipulated and used. It's a question of who has the stronger will.

The Prince...or his father.

"You know it was his idea to enslave us and trap us down here. Yet you hesitate to condemn his actions."

The Prince's eye twitches. "He's my father. I know he's not perfect, but he cares...in his own way. And it wasn't just his idea, for the record. It was the Council's."

I scoff, "And you think they challenge him? They pander to him. Wake up, Nyall Drayven. Wake up and see the truth."

"I do see the truth," he growls.

His anger sparks my own fire, and I want to rise to meet it.

But the hatchling is almost done feeding, and then it will want to sleep.

I cannot abandon it.

"You will," I nod. "Thank you for the food."

Nyall shakes his head, frustrated. "Yeah, whatever."

He walks away, leaving me in quiet.

I do not know why, but there is something about him.

Something I cannot place.

I feel Great Livyathin's claws tugging me towards the Prince. Asking me to trust, despite my head and my heart screaming at me not to.

Then a sound breaks through the silence, echoing through the hatchling stables.

The sound of another egg hatching.

Livyathin felt the doubt in my heart and sent a reminder.

The hatchlings will die if they do not feed. Which means I must trust the Prince.

Their lives depend on it.

The Prince returns the next day with more food and another pig. Then he returns the day after that.

And the day after that.

All five eggs hatched, and the Prince brought more bottles. Soon they'll begin to play, sleeping less and less.

They cannot live here forever.

Dragons are only small for the first year of their life.

Luckily at this age, hatchlings don't do much other than sleep and eat.

But I *am* concerned about what happens next.

One evening, just as Prince Nyall goes to leave after bringing milk for the hatchlings and a dead sheep for me, guards appear.

Nyall freezes and I immediately grab the hatchlings, pulling them close. I sink down into the shavings, hiding as much as possible.

"Prince Drayven. What are you doing here?" the Guard asks.

Nyall's face is hard before relaxing. A smirk appears on his lush pink lips.

"How amusing. Do you think you're in charge here? As if I owe you, a lowly guard, *anything?*" Nyall laughs and the guard flinches as if struck.

Interesting.

Very interesting.

They bow their heads.

"I'm sorry, milord," the head guard says, his voice trembling.

"You will tell no one you saw me here, or else I will feed you to this Dragon. Understand?"

I want to roll my eyes but instead, I rise out of the shavings and bare my teeth, growling at the guards.

The anger is always there, ready for the taking.

"We understand," the guard gulps.

"Good. You're dismissed."

I watch as the guards scurry away as fast as they can.

I've never been one for consuming mortals, but it takes everything in me not to chase after them.

I am a predator first.

"Fuck," Nyall curses as soon as they're out of sight. "That was close."

Shifting out of my Dragon form, I wait until my body shrinks, forming two legs, before striding out of the shavings.

I climb through the bars of the stable and approach Prince Nyall Drayven.

"Nothing stays secret here for long," the Prince runs his hand through his air, showing off his toned arms that strain beneath the fabric of his black runic. "Including you."

I nod, "You are correct. But the Fae are stupid"—Nyall glares at me, but I keep going— "they will not realize my stall is empty for some time. I would guess we have at least a few months, if not a year before they come looking."

Nyall shakes his head, "A year? You think you can hide down here for an entire year?"

I don't smile.

Nyall's face falls when he realizes I am serious.

"That means you need food for a year! I'll only be working down here for a little over two more weeks."

I step closer, until my chest is nearly touching his.

The Prince is taller than I expected, but I still tower over him.

His hair smells of honeysuckle and his skin of clean soap. It relaxes me, though I do not understand why.

"I guess I can sneak down here when the Citadel goes to sleep," Nyall gulps.

"Your heart is racing," my voice drifts into his thoughts.

At the sound of my voice, his heart beats even harder.

"You do realize you're naked?" Nyall asks aloud, his voice cracking slightly. "And a Dragon? You're everything I've been taught to fear. Of course, my heart is racing, I'm terrified!"

"I'm a Dragon," I remind him, *"I do not care for mortal drapes."* Nyall's breath shudders. *"Are you affected by me, Prince?"* I chuckle at the way his cheeks turn red.

"I am not," he hisses, the picture of righteous indignation.

"Well, I will agree that you are afraid," I say slowly. "But clearly, not afraid enough."

Nyall blinks, processing the true meaning in my words.

"You came back," I remind him. *"You're afraid, and yet here you stand. Toe to toe with a Dragon."*

Nyall looks up at me, his mouth open and his eyes wide.

"Yes," he whispers. "I am here."

"One year, Prince Drayven. I just need one year. Besides, it will benefit you to be owed a favor from a Dragon." I do not like begging, but I have no other choice.

I *need* his help. Desperately, in fact.

I'm so shocked I nearly fall over when the Prince nods, "Okay. One year."

"Will your father allow that?" I ask.

Nyall's eyes turn cold and hard. "I will say I can feel Sol Constantus calling me to service. To atone for my heretical behavior. He will have no choice but to agree."

How masterful he is at manipulation.

"I'll help," Nyall pauses, "if you tell me about Dragons. I want to know the truth. Not the lie we've so clearly been fed."

I'm not surprised he wants something in return.

But I *am* surprised at his request.

"Fine," I nod. "But you will swear a blood oath to never reveal what I share with another living soul."

His brows furrow.

He doesn't like this. I've put the Prince in a corner and it's up to him to decide what to do now.

"I'll do it," he says quietly. "I'll take the blood oath."

Nyall jerks as I wrap my arms around his shoulders and pull him into a hug.

"Thank you," I breathe. "Thank you."

Nyall's hands slide up my bare chest before pushing me away.

"I'm not doing it for you," he says, his brows furrowed. "I'm doing it because it's the right thing to do."

Nyall meets my eyes for one last second before turning and walking away.

A Fae Prince with a sense of morality. I never thought I'd see the day. Yet, when it came down to it, Prince Nyall protected us. He protected *me.*

One year. I have one year to raise the hatchlings. Once they're strong enough, I will help them escape.

Perhaps Nyall Drayven will be interested in assisting with that, too.

CHAPTER 5
NYALL

The weeks that followed were tense but easy.

However, things got more difficult once my time working in the Dragon Pit was over.

I had to sneak down in the middle of the night, which meant the hatchlings were already starving by the time I got there.

Keeping them fed was harder than I would ever admit to the Dragon, and six months into our little arrangement, the farmers have begun to grow *suspicious*.

"What are you doing here, Prince? More milk already?"

The farmer is Magyka. I can sense a bit of earth magyk about him. He was a tall male, and equally as wide.

Mr. Larousse was a keen male—*too* keen.

"It's at the High Council's request," I flash him an easy smile.

"How come it didn't go through the usual channels?" Larousse's hazel eyes narrow.

Shit.

Relaxing my face further, I shrug. "Your guess is as good as mine. It is not our place to question the actions of the High Council, Mr. Larousse."

Mr. Larousse glares, *tsking* lightly. "Prince Drayven, there is no reason the High Council needs *gallons* of sheep milk every night. I'm reporting this—"

I didn't want it to end up like this.

It wasn't supposed to be this way.

Mr. Larousse gasps as my dagger pierces his heart.

"I'm sorry," I whisper in his ear. "But you ask too many questions."

His body falls to the floor with a thud, sliding off of my dagger with a moist squelch.

Adrenaline rushes through my body, making my heart race and my hands tremble.

Sweat begins to drip down my back.

I glance between the bloody dagger and the dead body.

I killed someone.

Father was always talking about how I'm too soft. Too forgiving. How easily something soft can harden.

I hide the milk in the ether, keeping it out of sight. Dragging the dead body out of the farm, I weave a quick spell to make a hole in the ground. The magyk responds easily, like an excited puppy. It flows through me with a cool tingling sensation. In seconds, there is a large hole in the ground. I toss Mr. Larousse in and use a different spell to pour the dirt back into the hole.

I'm panting by the time I'm done. Magyk has come easily, yes, but I still have much to learn.

I bide my time until nightfall, when the Black Citadel grows quiet as the High Council goes to bed. I sneak away, climbing hundreds of stairs down into the Dragon Pit.

I find the Dragon and the hatchlings in their nursing stable, tucked away. As always, the Dragon has the hatchlings hidden beneath the shavings, along with its own, gigantic body. I grab the milk from the ether, along with an old cow I slaughtered. The Dragon grabs the milk and quickly feeds the crying hatchlings.

Even with my help, they're still so skinny.

The black Dragon even more so.

"I killed a man today," I say, my voice hollow.

The Dragon pauses, looking at me.

"Is this the first life you've taken, Prince?"

I nod.

Perhaps Father is right. Maybe I am too soft if I'm so easily read.

The Dragon huffs as he feeds another hatchling. They suckle the milk down so fast, their small, shining eyes turning glassy and sleepy as their bellies grow full.

"I have taken many lives, but I will always remember my first." The Dragon's voice is casual, but I feel an edge of regret.

I don't know when, but at some point, the adrenaline leaves my body and my shaking grows worse.

Tears begin to stream down my face as I picture Mr. Larousse. I can't stop thinking about the sound of his body hitting the ground. Quiet tears turn into sobs, the sound filling the stable, when all of a sudden, thickly muscled arms wrap me in a hug, pulling me close.

He shifted to...comfort me?

"You are right." The Dragon's voice is next to my ear. "Not all Fae are bad. What you feel right now? It's normal. Never lose this empathy, Prince Drayven."

I sniff, leaning my forehead on his shoulder. His skin is warm and smells of smoked vanilla and leather.

It's delicious.

"I don't regret it," I tell him, my voice muffled. "Helping you, I mean. What scares me is…" I pause, lowering my voice further out of shame, "What scares me is how easy it was, and how I didn't feel anything at all."

The Dragon takes a deep breath and squeezes me gently before pulling away, his golden eyes bright with an emotion I cannot define.

"It's terribly easy to kill and to die," the Dragon says slowly. "But what is necessary is often terrible."

"What is your name?" I blurt out, realizing I still do not know. "I have simply been calling you the Dragon."

The male snorts.

"Among my kind, I am known as a Beastkyn. A Dragon who chose to shift into mortal form. It's considered a sin."

"But your name isn't Beastkyn," I guess.

"No, it is not," the male chuckles and shakes his head. "My name is Remus Ostia, but my people call me Os."

"Os," I breathe. "It suits you."

"You sound surprised," Os crosses his arms and I try not to stare at his thick cock hanging between his legs.

He's always so *naked*.

"I always assumed Dragons would have quite complex names. But yours is rather human."

Os scratches his head, "Yes, it is. My sire was fond of mortals. I do have a longer name that cannot be pronounced in your basic tongue, but I prefer Os."

"You have your own language?" I ask. The hatchlings begin crying again and Os walks back into the shavings, cuddling them into his arms and whispering. I follow, sitting on the edge. One of the hatchlings approaches me, crawling on two legs and using the claws on its wings as support.

I sit and talk with Os for hours. After cleaning stalls, my midnights are spent hearing stories of the legendary creatures and their homeland on Elysium. It's like that every night for the next five months, but at the arrival of the eleventh month, everything changed.

CHAPTER 6
OS

The Prince is not what I expected. At every turn, he has proven to be the very opposite of his evil father.

I've found myself, for the first time in over a century, feeling an emotion that I thought long impossible.

Trust.

I trust Prince Nyall Drayven. I trust a *Fae.*

Deep down, a voice inside of me screams that this is a mistake. But I ignore it, suffocating it within my black claws.

He is not his father. He is better. *Kinder.*

I can see it in his soul, taste it in the purity of his Magyk. The time weighs heavy on my mind, and worry grows. I don't know how I will keep the hatchlings alive much longer.

The year of Prince Nyall's help is almost up.

Milk appears out of thin air as Nyall turns the corner. Two dead sheep follow. I hurry to feed the crying hatchlings before digging into the sheep.

The Prince carefully walks around the gate to find the brief section without any metal bars blocking the way. He sits down at the edge, dragging his feet through the shavings.

It feels so casual. There is a surety in his movements and demeanor that strikes me.

The Prince does not think he is brave, but it's been many years since I've seen a Fae, let alone a mortal so comfortable in my—or *any* Dragon's—presence.

Blood covers my snout, but I don't bother cleaning it before shifting into mortal form. My scales disappear, hiding beneath thin, umber-colored skin.

"What are you going to do? At the end of the month?" Nyall asks.

I shrug, "I do not yet know. But I will figure it out. I have no other choice."

"How did you get out of your stall, by the way? I never did ask."

I smirk. "They never caught me in the first place. I snuck in before the captives were brought down here and hid. I was going to help them all escape until I found the eggs…" I look down at the hatchlings as warm affection rises within me. "I couldn't leave them," I whisper.

"You are brave," Nyall says. "Far braver than I."

"I don't know about that," I glance at him. "You are defying your father by helping me. You've smuggled food for us for almost a year straight. That is very brave."

Nyall's smile is warm and shy.

He's young.

So young.

And so beautiful already.

At a century? Or two? He will be devastating.

"What are you thinking about?"

I meet his mismatched gaze.

One of amber, and one of green.

His eyes were so hypnotizing. So unique. I couldn't look away.

I wade through the shavings until my arms are on either side of Nyall's legs.

His cheeks grow pink at my proximity, something which pleases me greatly.

I am like most Dragons. I do not love based on gender.

We mate with and love whomever we wish. As long as they're *also* a Dragon, of course.

I've never been one to follow the rules.

Nyall's eyes are wide and his breath still as I lean in and brush my nose against his.

Our lips are so close, I can feel the heat wafting off his skin, can taste his breath on my tongue.

The Prince leans in but I pull back. I will not take advantage of the younger Male.

He might feel like an adult, but I am 1,500 years old. At 30, he has only *just* matured.

The Prince doesn't even know himself yet. But I leave that to Great Livyathin to decide.

"I will miss you, when the month is through," Nyall blurts.

Well.

How unexpected.

Shocked, I stare at him, trying to find any ounce of deception. But there is none.

Just honesty.

How refreshing.

I smile, despite the terrible circumstances we're in. "And I, you."

I did not plan to say that. But the sentiment is surprisingly true. Despite my every effort, I have become rather fond of the Prince. His daily visits bring light into this dark, dreary place.

Nyall leans in, not to kiss me but to rest his forehead against mine.

I lean into him as well, our arms tangled. The hatchlings curl around our legs, content and warm.

"I wish we could stay like this," Nyall admits.

So do I.

So do I.

CHAPTER 7
NYALL

Oh Gods.

Why the fuck did I just say that?

Os snorts, his hand cupping my cheek. "You need to work on hiding your emotions. You're so easy to read."

I raise a brow, "Perhaps you're just a Dragon."

His head tilts back and he lets out a deep laugh.

Oh. That *sound.*

My heart races in the presence of that sound.

"Would you—" I hesitate, taking a deep breath. "Would you tell me a story?"

Os tilts his head, the action so other it reminds me that while he wears the form of a mortal male, he is not. He is all Dragon.

"A story?"

I nod. "Or just...tell me about your life."

Os blinks.

Ugh, I'm making a mess of this.

"It has occurred to me, that what we have been told about Dragons is, erm, likely not true," I clear my throat, "I do not wish to know your secrets, for those are yours to keep. But I would like to know the truth, at least."

"Hm," Os nods. "Yes, in that you are correct. What you have been told is not true. I will not tell you anything that can be used against my kind, but I will tell you about my homeland."

"Your home?" I ask.

"Yes," Os smiles. "Elysium. Your kind would not be able to get there, so it is safe to discuss."

"Do you miss it?"

Os looks away, his smile fading. "I...I do. But for many years, I did not."

"How long has it been? Since you've been home?"

We settle in as Os continues talking.

"It's been over a century since I left Elysium. Perhaps more. Time is...difficult to track when you are as old as I am. I came here before your people arrived."

He says "people" with a growl, the resentment clear in his voice.

"I am sorry," I whisper.

Os's head snaps towards me. "Was it your decision to come here? To break our world and take over this Kingdom?"

"I—uh, no." I stammer.

Os bares his teeth. "Then do not apologize for something that is not your fault."

Right.

Os takes a deep breath and continues. "Arkaydia used to be home to many Dragons. I visited here many times, but I decided to stay here permanently just before your people arrived."

"Why did you leave?" I ask gently, feeling somehow like the answer is sensitive and difficult for the Dragon to discuss.

Os looks away again.

"I was...not welcome anymore."

Wait, what?

"What I am," he gestures to his mortal form, "is not accepted by my kind. When I decided to take this shape and shed my Dragon form, my people began to turn on me. They feel that Dragons are the superior species. To shift away from that form is to tarnish that which is already perfect. I could have stayed but...they were set on making my existence miserable if I had done so. So I left my family, my home, and everything I've ever known and came here."

"That's horrible," I breathe, "Os I'm so sorry."

He shrugs. "I do not regret it. They do not see that being able to take multiple forms is a strength, and that nothing in this wretched world is perfect. Not even a Dragon."

Wow.

"You said you left your family behind?"

Os nods, a sad smile on his face. "My sister. I hated leaving her, but she's a Dragon. Not Beastkyn like me. She's far away from here, safe in Elysium where our people will protect her. Now I am grateful for the distance. Knowing she is alive and safe is a comfort."

"What's her name?" I ask, curious to know more but not wanting to push too hard.

Os meets my gaze and reaches his hand up, brushing my white blonde hair off my brow.

"Embyrne," he says. "Her name is Embyrne."

"That's a beautiful name. Is she a Black Dragon like you?"

He laughs, "No. I am somewhat of an anomaly. Black Dragons are very rare, but Embyrne...she is even rarer. She's a gold Dragon."

I gasp, "A *gold* Dragon? I've never heard of such a thing."

"She's beautiful. With scales of pale gold and deep, golden eyes. Our mother was a gold, the first gold to be born in a thousand years."

My mind is racing with all of this new information. "So some....*colors* are more common than others? Is each color of Dragon its own species?"

Os laughs. "One question at a time."

We spend the rest of the night talking. Telling each other about our lives. I could listen to his stories forever.

I wish this year would never end.

"Nyall, get down here. I have something to tell you!" Father shouts down the hall.

I finish dressing and leave my room, making my way to Father's sitting area.

I enter through the double doors, and find my father seated behind a black marble table. Statues of the Fae leaders who died in the Great War line the room, along with statues of Achan himself.

It always struck me as a bit odd, having a statue of oneself in their own rooms.

"Father," I greet him with a nod. He waves a hand at me to sit down, his black nails sharpened into dagger-like claws.

I take a seat, the wood and metal chair scraping on the floor as I settle myself. "What news?"

I don't know why, but I find my father's reaction to this very disturbing.

He smiles. He *never* smiles.

"I've had a vision."

I blink, "A vision?"

Achan smiles wider, his white fangs flashing in the light. "Yes. A vision. From Constantyn himself. I've consulted the Archmage and he agreed; He sent me a vision."

"What was the vision about?" I ask, curious...and completely on edge. Adrenaline rushes through me. Something about this feels wrong, but I do not know why.

"The vision was about...repentance."

"Repentance?" My voice is laced with confusion and concern.

"Yes. So many of the Arkaydian rebels survived. Humans, mostly," Achan's upper lip curls in disgust. "But our God has shown me how we will ensure their little rebellion never happens again."

I wait, terrified as to his next words.

Achan smiles wider, "We're going to have a tournament. I'm thinking of calling it...***The Gauntlet.***"

CHAPTER 8
NYALL

The next night, I take milk down to Os as usual.

The hatchlings were crying, whining and hungry, and Os is restless because of it. I get into the stall, kneeling in the shavings as I help him feed the young Dragons. They're still very small, but they're too big for me to hold. Most of them are about the size of a large dog.

Soon, they'll begin to grow at a rapid rate.

Or at least that's what Os said.

I summon the cow I had slaughtered earlier, and Os digs in. His snout is covered with blood.

When he finishes, his eyes grow warm and relaxed. A split, serpentine tongue flicks out as he tastes the blood left on his scales.

I can't help but raise my hand and place it on his cheek.

His scales are soft and warm.

He's so magnificent.

I am in awe.

I smile at him, and he leans into me, pressing his snout against my cheek.

Which is when a voice calls from behind us.

We both go still, bodies and hearts frozen.

I turn, seeing the world in slow motion, as I take in the sight of my father.

"Well, now. This is a creative idea, son."

What the fuck is he doing?

"I do not know what you mean, Father," I respond, stepping away from Os. I climb out of the stable and make my way to Father's side.

Focus on me.

Focus on me, and not them.

I try to draw his attention, but it doesn't work.

Father merely glances at me with a smirk, "Very creative, indeed. Tell me, how did you manage to trap the Beastkyn? You've seen him shift, surely."

My heart stops.

Fuck.

FUCK.

"Why are you here?" I blurt, trying to distract him.

Father glances at me with disdain. "Don't embarrass yourself. I've been spying on you since the moment you learned how to walk and talk."

I...*what?*

"You've been spying on me?"

Father laughs, but there is no humor in it. "I know better than to trust my own son."

Hurt *burns* in my blood as my Father turns his attention back to the Dragon.

"Now, tell me about your scaled friend. He can shift, then? How interesting."

I scramble to downplay the situation. "It was...a freak occurrence. I've been monitoring him, ensuring he isn't a threat."

Father's eye twitches.

He knows I'm lying.

"No," his voice is deadly, making my knees weak and wobbly. "No, I do not think it was. But I don't actually care. You brought me what I needed."

Father looks at Os and smirks as guards file in behind us.

I look around, frantic, unable to breathe.

No. Fuck!

The guards surround the stable and I realize that in their hands are nets.

Small nets.

My heart shatters. Breaking into a thousand tiny pieces.

"Father, I—" I break off.

There's no point.

Os looks at me, his gold eyes burrowing a hole into my soul.

I want to defend him, but I can't. That will only end up with *both* of us six feet under.

But a crazy idea forms in my head.

A horrible, terrible idea; but one that will keep us both alive, and Os is going to *hate* me for it.

CHAPTER 9
OS

I knew before he spoke the words that Nyall Drayven had decided to betray me.

"This *tournament*," Nyall says slowly. "You will need a trainer who will prepare the candidates for it. Who understands Dragons. After all, we want to put on a good show. That means they need to know how to fight and how to kill."

I cannot help it. I am, after all, a Dragon.

With a snarl, I launch myself at them, using my wings to propel me straight at Achan.

Nyall is faster. He uses his fancy magic, light bands encircling his arms as I'm suddenly thrown into the air. I hit the back wall so hard, I see stars.

Achan is there a second later, hovering over me.

A new voice sounds, "Ah good. I've arrived just in time."

Achan's red magic suddenly surrounds me, wrapping around my body like rope. It burns and I shriek, writhing against it.

"Shift, and the pain stops," Achan purrs.

The pain increases and I cave.

They need to focus on me, not the hatchlings.

Naked and sweaty, I lay on the ground breathing heavily.

"That's better. Now," the Archmage appears next to Achan. "This will only hurt for a moment."

I've only seen him from afar. But up close, the male is so perfect it's unnerving. His hands light up with purple fire, something I've never seen before.

Then his words hit me, and at the same moment, his hands touch my bare skin and that purple fire burns.

I roar, reaching for my Dragon form, as my hands grow black claws.

But that form is...far away, and growing further away by the second.

The Archmage weaves a spell of Death into my skin, one that erases my other side. I can *feel* my Beast retreating. Locking me in this form.

Leaving me broken. One piece of a whole.

Tears crawl down my cheeks as I begin to lose consciousness.

The last thing I see is Nyall Drayven's face, his eyes full of regret.

Then the world turns to darkness, and I am *lost*.

CHAPTER 10
NYALL

Something breaks in me that day.

Something *permanent.*

I watch, unable to do anything as my father and the Archmage torture Os. The spells the Archmage burns into the Dragon's mortal skin are spells I've never seen before. I don't recognize any of the symbols.

But I can feel what it is they do. They're caging him. Locking his Beast away...and tethering him to the city. I feel the way the spell burrows down into the Earth. Holding him here within the confines of the Pit.

He will never be able to leave.

What have I done?

Oh God, what the fuck have I done?

Eventually, my father and the Archmage leave. They instruct the guards to take the hatchlings and carry Os out. I follow behind. Every step is torture as the hatchlings scream and struggle against the woven nets.

I don't want to know where they're taking them. But I fear.

"You did this," the voice is so venomous, I almost shrink away. A glance ahead and I meet Os' gold eyes. *"This is your fault. You did this."*

He's gone before I can say anything else. Father has him brought into the Citadel and we follow, ever the dutiful court.

Each step fills me with dread. My heart races, thumping against my chest bone so hard I might shatter.

We're brought into a small room, and I'm surprised to see the other High Councilors are present.

"Father, what is—" I ask but a hand slaps my cheek.

"Be quiet!" Father snaps at me, furious. "Hold your tongue and be silent, boy."

I look at the ground, ashamed, my cheeks burning in pain and embarrassment.

But...I don't understand. I want to scream at him. To tell him this is wrong.

Deep down, I know that would only mean my end.

The nets are placed on the table; one in front of each Councilor.

Something is wrong. Something is so very *wrong*.

My heart races as the blood rushes through my body. Each High Councilor produces a dagger.

That's when Os starts to scream. Heart-wrenching, soul-deep screams so loud, I can hear as the fray his vocal cords.

They're screams of *grief.*

I watch in horror as the Councilors plunge their daggers into the hatchlings, butchering them and tearing their bodies apart, before they bring the bloody limbs and organs to their mouths.

They...*eat* them, and I can't look away. Not because I'm jealous, nor because of hunger or gluttony, but because it's impossible to believe that this is real. I keep pinching my arm until it's bruised and bleeding, hoping that this isn't real. That this is just a bad dream and any moment I will wake up.

WAKE UP. WAKE UP! I scream in my head, begging Constantyn to save me.

And yet, it is real—and it doesn't stop.

The Councilor's laugh as they consume every bit of the hatchlings in front of them, their faces coated in Dragon blood.

Father turns to me, and I nearly throw up in horror as he hands me a piece of the bloody meat. I shake my head and Father shrugs, before taking a big bite of it.

Os continues to scream, the sound turning hoarse as he shreds his own vocal cords. Then those screams turn into sobs. Great, heaving sobs of such pure, undiluted pain that I begin to cry too.

Father's hand punches me in the back of the head so hard, my face is slammed down onto the table. Pain explodes throughout my face.

"Fucking pathetic," he whispers. "You're an embarrassment."

His hatred dries my tears.

No.

No, I am not in the wrong.

He is.

I will not give my Father the pleasure of seeing me weak. My tears dry up and I swallow any moans of pain, sitting up straight in my chair.

Stars still twinkle at the edge of my vision from the injury to my head, but I do not move.

Father sneers at me, watching as the tears continue to dampen my burning cheeks. "Dragons are animals, son. These are not emotional, intelligent beings. They are trash, meant only to be used, and we, my son, we are the users. They are our tools."

He keeps talking but I tune him out—my father is wrong. I have seen their intelligence. I have seen that Dragons love just as hard as we do. For the first time in 30 years, I cannot shake the feeling that I'm being lied to. I have felt it before, but I smothered it, suffocating any feelings of doubt within my bare hands.

That doubt unleashes within me, and for once, I let it go free.

Every whisper, every rude comment, every punishment and slap, every single time I've ever heard someone call my father a monster—it all runs through my head. Over and over again the memories play in my thoughts alongside the Beastkyn's screams.

Monster.

Monster.

The truth is heavy. I feel the weight of realization as the truth finally arrives. A truth I've avoided and denied my entire life.

My *father* is the monster.

Not the Dragons.

Not the Arkaydians or the humans.

Him.

And this *God* he makes us pray to—that god doesn't exist.

Constantyn, the Gods; it's all a pretty lie.

What *God* would allow this to happen?

Any *love* I ever held for my Father dies with those hatchlings. Any *belief* I ever held for a higher power is distinguished alongside Remus Ostia's freedom.

The only thing that remains clear and true is that no matter how much time passes, I know in my heart of hearts, Remus Ostia will never forgive me for this.

Never.

CHAPTER 11
OS

Year 25 PBM

I thought I knew the depths of the Fae's depravity.

It turns out, I knew nothing of it. I merely saw the surface.

It's been 11 years since I watched Achan Drayven consume my kind. Every year, I've sunk deeper and deeper beneath the surface.

It's been 10 years since I was forced to train a group of unruly, unprepared humans to fight in the Gauntlet—I watched them all *die.* All but one.

The survivor was not the best fighter, nor the smartest. The survivor was the one who took the most lives.

I knew the second I heard the screams and roars of the boisterous crowd that the Gauntlet was only the beginning. After the first Gauntlet, Achan Drayven showed up at my cell a few months later and announced another kind of game.

The *Fray.*

Not a tournament, but a fight to the death.

The Fray would happen monthly.

The best of Ur Daoine's fighters would come together and battle it out for the title of Champion; though the title would only truly be achieved if they won the final bout—a fight to the death against a Dragon.

The crowd roars in the distance, ripping me out of my memories.

My mortal skin feels tight, as if my Beast is tearing through my body, ready to be unleashed.

The magyk cuffs didn't last long; my Beast was too strong. So instead, Achan had the Archmage create some sort of cursed ink. Compulsion magyk broken down and mixed with pigment. They tattooed glyphs in the Fae language all over my torso, glyphs that lock me in my body, separating me from my beast forevermore.

"BEAST. BEAST. BEAST. BEAST!" The crowd screams my name.

I'm waiting in a dusty tunnel, only just hidden from the crowd's sight. Bloody handprints and trails line the tunnel. Reminders of the death that happens here.

My body is alive, but my soul died a long time ago. As the tunnel gate is lifted and I'm given the signal to enter the Arena, I prepare to commit the gravest of sins, killing my own kin.

CHAPTER 12
NYALL

My heart races as I watch Os walk onto the Arena sand. Pools of blood decorate the ground where the past combatants met their end at the tip of Remus Ostia's blade.

I've watched him do this before, but the anxiety never leaves no matter how many times these events repeat.

A shiny, silver helmet covers his head.

He's shirtless, showing off his muscled physique, but I cannot take my eyes off the tattoos covering his skin.

Father *bound* him.

I watched the Archmage create the goddamn ink myself.

I've wanted to stop them at every step, but I cannot.

Their magyk is simply much stronger than mine.

In a few centuries, if I should live that long, that reality might change, but I'm just over 100 years old, where the Archmage is practically a historical *relic*. I've never asked how old he is, nor how old Father is, but I would guess both are nearing the thousand-year mark.

Which means I cannot challenge them. Not yet.

The Archmage is simply a pawn anyways, he does what he is told, no more, no less.

But my father...

My father is a different story. For 100 years, I have watched his cruelty grow.

As Remus Ostia takes a fighting stance and unsheathes his blade, I find myself wondering if this will ever end. This reign of terror.

A gate lifts at the opposite side of the Arena to where Os is standing, and a big cloud of smoke rushes out.

I expect the Dragon to be big.

But it's small; and it's fucking *injured.*

The Dragon that emerges is a light copper color. I'm sure at one point, its scales were resplendent and metallic, but now their color has seeped away, leaving a dull, orange-brown shade behind.

But it's wings. *God,* it's wings.

One of them is bent backwards, the joint broken in half. I can see the white bone poking through the thin skin of the wing membrane.

They didn't even heal it before making it fight for its life. I don't dare look at my father right now, nor the other High Councilors, but in my head, I scream at them.

Os doesn't hesitate. He simply watches the Dragon approach, its blue eyes wide and terrified.

I hate this.

I hate all of this, and most of all, I hate my father for causing it.

The Dragon is dragged into the arena, chains around its two legs.

I've learned over time that Dragons can either have two legs or four. The ones with two legs have sharp claws at the end of their wings, and they use those claws like another set of limbs for balance.

Dragons with four legs have smaller, clawless wings. The copper Dragon in the Arena below can barely walk, due to the broken wing.

The crowd boos at it, throwing rotten fruit at its head. The Dragon cries out, terrified and in pain. It shrinks away as the Fae attendants take off the chains and metal muzzle around its snout. There is a large *thunk* as it all falls to the ground. The attendants run out, abandoning the Dragon to its fate.

The Dragon tries to follow them, but the gate shuts, locking it in the Arena. A loud ringing sound goes off, projected and enhanced with a spell.

"BEGIN!" my father calls with a faux-benevolent wave at the crowd.

As Os approaches the Dragon, I grip the arms of my seat so tightly, the metal groans. The Dragon blinks at him, clearly recognizing what Os hides within his mortal coils.

Then Os is beneath the Dragon, his sword slicing through the Dragon's throat.

It should be a quick death, but the Dragon cries out in pain, struggling as its blood spills onto the sand in a steaming pool.

Os screams as he slices his sword across its neck again, severing the Dragon's head completely.

The crowd goes silent for a beat, before erupting in raucous cheers.

"BEAST! BEAST! BEAST!"

Os turns around and takes his helmet off. Those gold eyes are burning bright, and they're staring straight into mine.

It's quick.

A mere moment.

Then his eyes slide to the side, landing on Father.

The scream that explodes from Os' mouth is like a blade slicing through my heart.

The pain. The sorrow. The *fury.*

There is no end.

Only a gyre, circling and circling as the same path repeats itself over and over again.

The same *pain.* The same *loss.*

His loss...and mine.

CHAPTER 13
NYALL

"Well, well. If it isn't the Heretic Prince," a voice laughs. "Welcome, milord, to my humble abode."

The barkeep lets out a laugh as the denizens sitting throughout the alehouse join in.

There is no way to hide who I am. I'm too easily recognized.

It's my own fault, I suppose. The first time I publicly challenged my father, I was 150 years old.

It took me a century and a half to get the courage to do so.

He punished me by claiming my rebellion, my *distrust*, was a "Sin to Constantyn."

In front of the entire court and all of his advisors, I smiled told him that his, "God could go fuck himself," and that Constantyn "didn't exist."

First, he beat me.

Then he had someone fetch the Archmage as guards pinned me down.

The Archmage showed up, his face emotionless as ever.

Then my teacher, my *guide,* proved he's little more than another slave to my Father's whims.

The Archmage tattooed me, infusing the ink with his purple magyk.

59

My so-called teacher didn't even hesitate as he carved the word into my skin with his scalpels and tools, peeling my skin away with horrible precision and then wiping the ink over the raw, bleeding skin.

The word is permanently inked across my throat for all to see. The court watched the beating with greed in their eyes. Almost salivating at the sight of my blood and my pain.

All would know that I rejected Sol Constantus, and Sol Constantus rejected me.

"Fucking pathetic," Father whispered in my ear as I groaned in pain at the feeling of the ink sinking into the raw wound. "Pathetic and unworthy of the gifts you've been given."

Father stands and turns to address the crowd as the Archmage finishes the job.

"I declare for the realm to see, that you, Nyall Drayven, are a heretic, and are no heir or son of mine. You're just another bastard. A *mistake.*"

Any love I once held for the male was long gone, but that was the nail in the coffin for us. Since that day, I have spent every single day hating him.

I'm awfully tired of watching as he destroys Ur Daoine and everyone in it. The barkeep wordlessly pours me a large cup of mead.

Alcohol only drowns the misery for a moment. Not long enough to make much of a difference.

After a few hours of drinks and politely turning down suitors, I head back home.

The Black Citadel; my pretty birdcage. Just as I close in on the moat and get ready to walk across towards the Citadel, a voice nearby catches my attention.

I know that voice.

Keeping to the shadows, I peer through the bushes and look out onto the entrance to the Dragon Pit.

Os.

Regret is a heavy blanket on my shoulders.

There's much I regret in this life, but what happened with Os and the hatchlings that day...that is the heaviest regret of all.

For the past 250 years, I've wanted the chance to explain.

To tell him he was right about my father...to finish the kiss we left unfinished. A kiss that keeps me up at night at the mere thought of it. I still remember the feeling of his lips against mine, of his *heat*, burning like my own inferno.

So, I follow him.

As Os goes back into the Dragon Pit, I follow, quiet and unnoticed. I've gotten rather good at that.

I will never admit how many times I've studied the blueprints of this place, memorizing the location of his room and imagining where he is throughout the day.

Is this obsession?

~~YES. BUT I DON'T CARE.~~

He hasn't noticed I'm behind him yet. Just as he goes to open his bedroom door, I call out.

"Wait."

The male pauses, his neck swiveling back while his body remains planted, like an owl. It was terrifying.

Not as terrifying, though, as Remus Ostia up close. Those golden eyes burn holes into my very soul as he gazes at me.

His stare strips me naked.

"What do you want, Prince Drayven?"

He says my name the same way someone screams, "FUCK!" when they stub their toe. With righteous fury.

"I was hoping we could talk."

"You hope?" Os scoffs. "Why would I give you even a moment of my time? Unless it's an order, *Prince.*"

The air turns hot with his blistering questions.

He's right. I know he is.

"I will never order you to do *anything.*"

His eyes narrow, distrust plain within them.

"Fine. Come in and say what you have to say so that we can go another two centuries without speaking."

Fuck.

Each word is a blade slicing into my skin. We enter his room, a cozy space full of wooden and leather furniture.

We head towards a grouping of chairs by the crackling fireplace. I take a seat on one of them, sinking into the plush leather.

He on the other hand, remains standing, leaning against the wall.

Fine.

I flash him my now signature smirk. "Do take a seat, please. You're hovering."

"It is my room," he growls. "I may do what I please."

I shrug, "And it's my kingdom."

Os slowly looks down at my neck and the word now branded there. His eyes lift, meeting my own, and he flashes a smirk of his own.

"Is it?"

My heart stops for a moment. I look away, concentrating on the flames instead. I've always liked the blue part of fire the most. The way the flames only get when they're burning hot, turning for a brief moment to bright blue and navy, before fading back into orange and red.

"No," I answer finally. "It's not."

"Ah, is this why you've come?" Os nods, but there is no kindness in him right now. "Poor lost Prince finally learned that Daddy is evil."

I stand and prowl over to him, anger a hot spark in my belly.

"Oh dear," he mocks. "Did I upset you? How terrible."

"Is this what you want?" I hiss. "You want me to tell you I should've listened when you said he was bad? Fine. You were right, Os. You were fucking right. Does that feel good to hear?"

He watches me, listening to my tirade, and his smirk only grows.

"Yes, actually. It does. You deserve the worst. You all do."

"Ask me," I snarl. "Ask me how my Dragons I've killed. You think I'm like them? Then prove it."

My shirt is in Os' hands a second later as he lifts me into the air and slams me against the wall. One hand leaves my shirt as I slide down to the ground. He grips my neck, squeezing just enough that it's uncomfortable.

"How many?"

He flashes a wicked set of fangs in my face, so close I can feel his breath on my skin.

"None," I breathe. "I have never killed a Dragon. Nor eaten one."

"You're lying," Os watches me, his brow furrowed.

"I am not," I force the words out despite his grip. "I never have, and I never will."

"You're *lying*." Os leans closer, so close our lips nearly touch.

Which is exactly when I realize his lower body is pressed against mine, and he can feel the way my cock grows harder by the second, straining against the fabric of my trousers.

"I'm not, and I'll swear it in blood that I will never harm a Dragon."

I can tell that shocks him by the way his eyes go wide and his fangs disappear.

"You would swear a blood oath?" he asks quietly.

"Yes," I stop suffocating my emotions and let them bleed into my eyes, showing him every ounce of regret within me. "I would, Os. Ask me to do it and I will."

He takes a deep breath, looking at me like I very well might be a stranger.

"It's been a long time. People change," I remind him, and his hand loosens around my neck. But he doesn't let go. Instead, his thumb caresses my neck, trailing lines on my skin. Goosebumps break out on my arms and my breath trembles.

"Some do," he admits. "But most do not."

We stand there, intertwined, staring into each other's eyes as the fireplace crackles beside us, casting the room and the Dragon before me in a golden glow. His gaze travels across my face, memorizing my features.

I do not look like the boy I once was.

He, however, hasn't changed at all. He's just as breathtaking as the day I met him.

Os' wavy black hair is slightly longer. It curls around his ears, teasing the nape of his neck.

His body, like mine, is covered in tattoos, but besides that?

"Os, I—" a knock on the door stops me and both our heads snap to look.

"Os? It's me," a feminine voice calls. *Ireyna.*

"I heard you took a lover," I note casually. "Another trainer from the program."

Os steps back, letting me go.

"I fuck who I please," he nods. "You've said your piece, now I'll say mine: get out."

A part of me knew this is what was going to happen, that this wouldn't change a damn thing. But it still hurts like hell.

"Thank you for hearing me out," I say quietly before walking past him and leaving.

I don't look back. I cannot.

There is no changing reality, and the reality is Remus Ostia will never forgive me. Our...*friendship* is long past.

I don't even spare a glance at Ireyna as I pass her, though I do catch the nasty glare she sends me. I keep walking until I exit the Dragon Pit, leaving Os and our time together behind in more ways than one.

***

"Back so soon?" The barkeep laughs until he gets a closer look at my face.

"Whatever it is, you need this." He pours me a fresh cup of mead and I down it in one go.

"Another," I say, my voice hoarse.

The barkeep nods. I hate the pity in his eyes as he looks at me.

Maybe I am the lost Prince.

Os has been right about everything else, why not that?

"Prince Drayven!" another voice calls as the barkeep passes me the freshly refilled cup of mead. I turn and look at one of the larger tables in the back. The voice seemed to come from there.

Someone waves, "Feel like a round of Maundy? Buy in is 10 coins!"

The alcohol begins to hit me, so I smile and nod as the table cheers. Grabbing my drink, I head over and take a seat at the head of the table, next to the dealer.

"Prince Drayven! Good to see you," the dealer nods as he shuffles and begins to hand out cards.

"Please, Jay. When I'm here, it's just Nyall. No ass-kissing allowed."

Everyone cracks up. I know all the players, except one.

Turning to my right, I meet pale green eyes.

"Hello, *just Nyall*," the woman smiles. There's a warmth about her. Red, tangled curls crown her shoulders. She has a generous, soft build.

The woman holds her hand out. I grab it, shaking it lightly.

Callouses line her palms. I blink in surprise.

This...is the hand of a warrior.

The corner of the woman's mouth twitches. "I'm Mirielle."

There's a slight accent to her voice. It's subtle.

"Eastlander?" I ask.

She nods.

"You're far from home," I note as the game begins.

"I'm looking for something," she says quietly.

We fall silent as the round continues.

To the surprise of everyone at the table, Mirielle wins. Then she wins *again*. Five rounds later and there's nearly a riot going on around us.

"Cheater!" someone screams, and others nod.

I raise a hand and they all fall silent.

"Come on, Nyall. She clearly cheated," the barkeep calls.

I meet his eyes. "I'll take care of it."

Mirielle protests, pulling against me with surprising strength as I grab her arm and drag her out.

I don't stop when we leave, instead I keep going until we reach a secluded area covered in shadows between two tall taverns. Then I let her go.

Mirielle backs up, looking at me with confusion. "You're letting me go?"

"Yes."

"Why?"

"Because you cheated," I smirk. "And you did it too well. Where you messed up was winning the first two rounds. You should have *almost* won, then swept them at the end."

Mirielle's jaw drops.

"You said you're here because you're looking for something," I recall her earlier words. "Tell me what you're looking for. Perhaps I can help."

She shakes her head, but I persist.

"Consider it payment for letting you go," I wink.

Mirielle's cheeks flush.

"I...can't tell you what I'm looking for," she says quietly.

"Why not?"

She takes a deep breath, "Because...it's about your father."

I freeze. "I see. What about him?"

"I'm not...looking for your father," she says carefully. "I'm looking for re-venge."

Interesting.

Very interesting.

"Let me guess, he is the one who wronged you?"

She nods, and I let out a heavy sigh.

"My father has wronged many people in his life. You are merely one of them."

Her brow furrows as she processes my words.

"You will not get your revenge. Many have tried. I have tried. It never works."

Mirielle's eyes go wide at the confirmation that I too want revenge against my father.

"Have you?" she asks quietly, but with a confidence that throws me off.

Have I really tried to get revenge against my father?

Mirielle nods, "Perhaps the others failed because they have what we do not."

Now it's my turn to be confused.

Mirielle's smile is a mere twitch at the corner of her mouth. "We are not alone."

"Two against the entire High Council?" I ask in disbelief. "No, absolutely not."

Mirielle looks away, unable to hide her smile this time.

"I know of more," she whispers into the wind. "*Many* more."

As do I, but I don't let her know that.

"What if the way to succeed…is by getting revenge together?"

This is insane.

I don't know if this woman's story is even true or if her name is really Mirielle.

But *something* in me says it's true.

That this is real.

The moment feels electric. Like we were meant to meet. Meant to have this conversation.

"What's that look for?" she questions.

I look up to the stars and let out a breath. The sky is glorious tonight.

"Perhaps you are right, Mirielle from the Eastlands."

"So…you'll help me?" she asks.

I laugh. "If you help me in return."

"What do you need help with?"

As I look up at the moons, a decision is made.

A decision that I feel will change the course of my life.

A decision to not sit back and watch the world burn, but to try to put it out; by killing the arsonist behind it all.

"Those friends of yours, the ones who feel similarly?" I meet Mirielle's gaze. "Tell them Prince Nyall Drayven wants to talk."

CHAPTER 14
VIRGYL

Year 420 PBM

There is a sense of foreboding about the forest today.

The trees whisper to me. They whisper stories of a Fae attack a few kilometers south.

Concern washes through me; a few kilometers is too close to risk it, but I need to know if the threat is mitigated.

My senior pack members follow behind as we scout the area.

It's the start of winter. Snow is only just beginning to fall, and the ground is crisp with morning frost. The earth crunches beneath my large paws.

A kilometer away and the scent of ash hits me. Several wolves with me sneeze, but I just run faster.

Ash.

Ash.

The air smells faintly herbal; spicy and cool. A particular scent. One I haven't smelled in an age.

What are you trying to tell me, old friend?

As if guided by Her hand, I arrive at a small clearing near a destroyed cabin. At first, I do not see anything other than piles of ash and charred wooden boards.

Then something on the ground moves.

A small, whimpering sound reaches my ears.

I pad over to the creature, unsure of what it is.

A wounded animal, perhaps?

I nudge it, rolling it onto its back, and nearly stop breathing as bright blue eyes look up at me. There's a hollow look to them, like the being is somewhere else.

"Daddy?" the child asks, reaching for me.

The second its hand touches my fur, I am hit with a bolt of pure energy.

An Arkaydian.

My thoughts race as I try to make sense of things.

A wounded, abandoned Arkaydian?

For a moment, the child's blue eyes change, and I feel as the emotions within it go from panicked to angry.

Navy and silver flames shimmer within the child's gaze, burning from within.

I understand now why you sent me here.

This is not random, no feat of chance. Hellfyre is Her domain, Her power.

This child is a message. The young thing is so skinny and clearly traumatized, so I pick it up by its hair the same way I carry my young—by the scruff of their neck—and carry it back to my home.

The pack has many questions, but mostly they are simply curious.

"What is this?" Syska asks in my head as I set the child down on the ground.

With a thought, I conjure a fireplace.

My magyk isn't what it used to be, but I can still make a fire.

"I do not know," I answer finally. *"But I know that I was guided to it for a reason."*

"You think it's Morrigyn?" Syska asks, and I nod. *"Then the child can stay."*

"You do realize this is my pack, female?" I grumble and Syska playfully snaps at my cheek.

"I am Alpha alongside you. It is our pack."

"You're so very lucky I adore you like the moons."

She lets out a wolfy laugh before laying down next to the child. It immediately curls into Syska's white fur.

As my mate cleans the child, gray hair emerges.

Not gray like an older mortal, but *true* gray, like the color of steel...or *ash.*

After a few days, it becomes clear that the child is a girl.

She doesn't say anything, not for a while.

But eventually, I connect to that bright, burning light within her, and *speak.*

"What is your name, child?"

The girl blinks, not at all surprised that I'm speaking in her head.

An Arkaydian, indeed.

"Amalia," the girl croaks, her voice crackly. "My name is Amalia."

"It's nice to meet you, Amalia," I lean forward and lick her cheek. *"My name is Virgyl."*

"But the stars that marked our starting fall away.

We must go deeper into greater pain, for it is not permitted that we stay."

— Dante Alighieri, 1265-1321.
The Divine Comedy: Inferno

PART TWO:
THE BRAVE

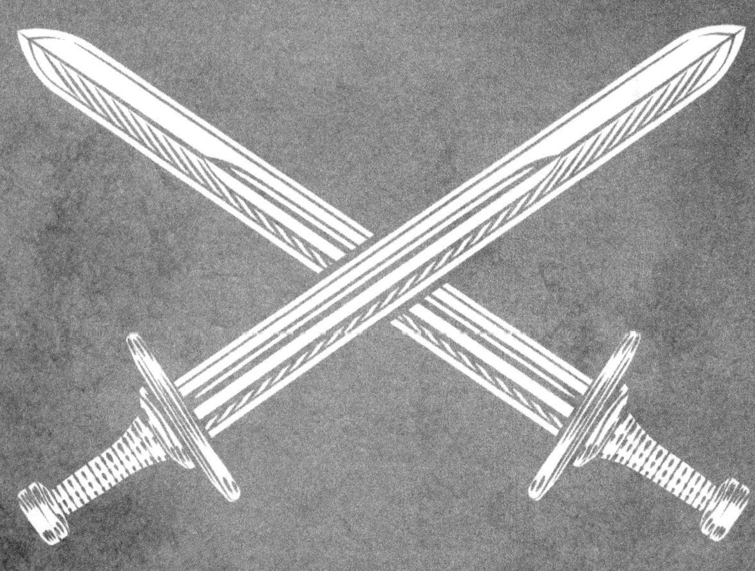

CHAPTER 15
AMALIA

Year 482 PBM

"What will you do with the girl?" Virgyl asks in my head.

The girl—Dyana—had just fallen asleep.

I never expected to find a lost little girl out in the woods this evening. When I realized what the small, crumpled up figure was, I almost fell over.

The moment she looked at me and smiled, despite the cold, despite the trauma of what she had just seen, my shriveled-up heart began to *thaw.* Just a little.

The pack surrounded her the moment I brought her back to the cave, their fuzzy bodies providing warmth and comfort.

"I don't know," I admit.

Virgyl pushes his nose into my hand and I snort, scratching behind his ears. His back paw slaps rhythmically as I dig my nails into his thick black fur.

"If you keep her, you will need to leave."

"No." The word echoes in my head. *"I will not leave."*

"Why not? Your kind are not meant to live alone in the woods, Blue."

"I don't want to leave. This is my home. The only home I've ever really known."

Virgyl chuffs, *"No one wants to leave home; yet still, they must. The time will come when the forest is no longer enough. The girl's presence will hasten that."*

"Keeping her doesn't mean I'll have to leave, Virgyl. I promise."

Virgyl falls quiet.

"As you wish," Virgyl says eventually. *"It is your choice. I will support whatever you decide to do."*

I look back at the girl, her black hair tangled and still damp from the rain. Her face is so peaceful.

I wish I felt that kind of peace.

"I can't abandon her," I whisper aloud, giving voice to my inner thoughts. "Not like—"

"—Like you were abandoned?" Virgyl finishes, and I nod. *"We will not abandon her. The girl pup can stay. She will be a part of our pack."*

I let out a deep breath, as if the weight of the world is on my shoulders.

Somedays it feels like it is.

"Maybe one day you'll even be friends," Virgyl teases.

I sniff and purse my lips. "I doubt it."

His wolfy laugh matches the beat of my heart.

"Her name is Dyana, by the way," I tell him. "That's what she told me."

"Dyana," Virgyl nods. *"A good name. An old name."*

I don't know about that, but I trust him. If the wolf says it's an old name, it is.

I just hope this wasn't a huge mistake.

CHAPTER 16
AMALIA

Year 487 PBM

"I'm sorry," Dyana whispers. "Ama, I'm so—"

"Hush," I stop her and wrap my arms around her in a loose hug.

She's almost taller than me. Not that I'm all that tall to begin with, but it feels like just yesterday that the top of her head only reached my belly button.

"This isn't your fault, Dy. Don't apologize."

"But...how else did those men find us?" Her voice trembles. "I'm the one who wanted to go into town."

I smile at her and brush my fingers across her tearstained cheek. "This isn't your fault. I do not blame you, Dyana. Those men weren't looking for you; they were looking for me."

"Okay, fine," she breathes. "But...can't we just stay in the forest?"

"No, we can't." I admit. "The forest and solitude might suit me, but my life will be long. Yours...will not."

Dyana frowns.

"Don't be sad. All I mean is, I want you to be a real human. Have a real human life. You deserve that, Dyana."

She wipes her tears.

I look around at the tall trees surrounding us. "I've stayed in the forest long enough. Besides," I meet her warm brown gaze, "sometimes the best place to hide is in plain sight."

Dyana furrows her brows. "I guess that makes sense."

"Come on, if we want to get to Österhamn by nightfall, we need to get going."

The pack is escorting us to the edge of the forest, and that is where our paths would part. I can't think about saying bye to Virgyl, or else I'll shatter into a million tiny pieces onto the damp forest floor.

"We'll find our home," I whisper to Dyana, grabbing her hand and squeezing. "I promise."

Year 490 PBM

"Gods, I hope this one works out," Dyana says, shivering against the cold. "Did you *have* to pick the coldest town in Ur Daoine though? Fucking hell."

I snicker. "Ten years in the forest and you *still* are such a baby about the cold."

She laughs alongside me, her cheeks pink from the frozen wind. "Yeah, you say that. Wait until your toes fall off, Roth! Then let's see who's laughing."

Her quips make me roll my eyes.

"I have a good feeling about this one," Dyana turns serious. "*Despite* the awful cold. I think this could be the one."

"I hope so," I breathe, fighting my own shivers against the cold as we walk into town, our light bags draped across our backs. "I really do.

Twyn Fells. The Northernmost town in Ur Daoine, and the most isolated. No one lives here by *choice*. They lived here because they needed space from the rest of the world. I just hope they leave me the hell alone.

We make our way to the inn. I saved some gold up from my old stable hand job, enough that we can stay there for a few nights while we both find work. The smell of warm berries and caramelized sugar hits me first. A fire crackles in the background, turning the air deliciously warm. The soft sound of conversation greets us.

It was busy, but not uncomfortably so. There was something cozy about the space.

The bottom floor was large, with a wooden staircase in the back leading up to three stories of rooms. A large counter to the left sat in front of the entrance to the kitchen. I could see pots and pans hanging above a simmering fire.

The smell of freshly baked bread hits me, making my mouth water.

"Hello, dears! Goodness, you two must be freezing." a warm voice calls as a head pokes out of the kitchen. Warm brown eyes greet us. A stout woman with brown curly hair peppered with gray approaches. Smile lines decorate her face; signs of a life well enjoyed.

"Did you walk all this way?" At our silence, she gasps. "Oh my. Sit down, sit down! My name is Mrs. Hunton. I'll make you some tea," she nods.

We gratefully take a seat on the tall stools at the wooden counter. The chairs creak, needing tending.

It's not a fancy inn, but it is clearly well loved.

Mrs. Hunton places two steaming cups of tea in front of us. The scent of cinnamon, pomegranates, and honey wafts toward me.

We pick up our mugs and each moan happily at the delicious taste. The tea was full-bodied and fruity; thick honey coats my throat, warming my body and soul.

"Thank you," I nod. "This is wonderful."

"It's my own recipe." Mrs. Hunton beams. "Now, what can I do for you young ladies?"

"We need a room for the night...and we're looking for work," Dyana says.

When confronted with normal socialization, I've developed a bad habit of clamming up.

"Work, hmm? I might be able to help. Many in the town visit my kitchen. In the evenings, we serve mead and ale; loose lips and all." Mrs. Hunton winks.

Maybe Dyana's right.

Maybe this will work out.

"I like to dance," Dyana smiles warmly. "Amalia works with horses, at the stables."

"Stables?" Mrs. Hunton turns to grin at me. "Ah. You prefer animals to people, don't you?"

I choke on my tea and Mrs. Hunton snorts. "Don't be embarrassed. I do not say that to judge. More to understand, because we just so happen to need a new stable hand. Our last one...well, he wandered off in the night and never returned. My husband has been tending to the beasts in the meantime."

I blink. "Oh. I can help with that. I have tended many stables in my life and I—I have a certain way with animals. They trust me."

It's the most I can say without divulging my magyk. If she is to be my employer, I need to impress her.

"I believe you," Mrs. Hunton smiles. "You should also know that the job would come in exchange of a free room here at the inn, and daily meals."

I nearly fall out of my chair. Instead, I merely give her a small nod. "I can *definitely* help with that."

She laughs, turning to Dyana. "I don't have a job for a dancer, unfortunately. But I do know that The Birdcage is only a few doors down. They're always hiring, and they provide lodging for their employees."

"Is it safe?" I ask pointedly. Dyana elbows me but I just swat her away.

Mrs. Hunton understands, though. "As safe as it can be."

"Very well," Dyana lifts her chin, the picture of bravery. "I'll go over there first thing tomorrow and inquire about a job."

"Good. In the meantime, rest. I'm sure your journey was long," Mrs. Hunton nods and glances back at the kitchen. "I'm the cook, too. Tonight is barley and vegetable stew. It's not fancy, but it's a local favorite. Shall I save you both a bowl and some fresh bread?"

Dyana nods so fast I'm surprised her head doesn't detach from her neck.

Mrs. Hunton hands us a key and we take our tea upstairs, only to immediately fall asleep.

The next day, Dyana and I split up. She heads down to The Birdcage while I make my way to the stables.

It's a simple building, but surprisingly well-kept considering the cold weather. Many of the stalls were empty, but a few held ponies with thick coats.

I stop at the last stall.

"Well. You are most certainly *not* a pony."

The huge horse nickers and shoves its huge gray head into my hands so hard that I nearly fall over.

A glance back confirms that it is a he.

"What's your name?" I ask, reaching one hand up to caress his cheek. His white fur is speckled with gray dots, but his snout, legs, and mane are midnight black. He's huge, with hooves nearly as big as my face.

I tentatively open my mind and reach out, searching his. We connect instantly and I feel his happiness at having a new friend. I can't hear words, but I can tell what he's feeling. I back up and he follows me, nibbling at my fingers. A name is carved onto a wooden sign at the front of his stall.

"Taran," I say aloud. The horse shoves his head into my hands again, rubbing up and down my chest in an attempt to get scratches. "Hello, Taran. It's nice to meet you."

He nickers again and I pull out the piece of apple I hid in my coat pocket. Horses are food motivated creatures. Taran licks my hand, scooping up the piece of apple in one swoop. Crunching happily, I smile as a wave of love and happiness is sent my way.

"Would you like to be friends?" I ask, before breaking out in rare laughter as he licks my cheek, covering it in slobber and bits of apple. "I'll take that as a yes."

"Ama?" a voice calls. "I got the job!"

Dyana's face appears as she walks through the stable. "Make a new friend?"

"Meet Taran," I introduce them, and he nibbles her fingers, hoping for treats. "You got a job? Just like that?"

Dyana nods, a small smirk appearing on her face. "They had me dance to one song and that was enough."

"They're not making you do anything untoward, right?" I ask, instantly suspicious.

Dyana chokes, "First off, no one says that anymore. You can say it. SEX."

I cringe.

"S. E. X." Dyana spells out, laughing at my embarrassment. "No, they're not going to make me have sex with the customers. That's not part of the job. It's just dancing. They can look, but that's all."

"Good, I'd hate to have to rip more tongues out."

Dyana blinks, "Yes, we really need to discuss your social skills. You can't just randomly maim and kill people."

Now it's my turn to blink.

"I will *try* not to hurt anyone," I say. "But should anyone hurt you, all bets are off."

"Alright, killer," Dyana snorts. Then her arms wrap around me and her head leans on my shoulder. She's taller than I am now, but she'll always be little in my eyes.

"Do you think this is it?" she whispers. "Is this...*home*?"

Taran nuzzles my hand, rubbing his forehead against me.

"Maybe," I force a smile onto my face.

It might be home for Dyana, but for me...I'm not sure I'll ever have a home.

CHAPTER 17
OS

Year 500 PBM

I hate this part.

I've been pretending for so long, I don't even have to think about it. The role comes so naturally. As the years pass, sanity leaves me, like shredding fabric. Every year, I lose another thread. Another piece of myself, gone to this place. It's eating away at me and soon...there will be nothing left.

The room beyond is filled with quiet conversation. I can hear all of it. I have to look 30 humans in the eye and tell them they're going to die. I have to pretend that the Fae gives two shits about them when this is all for sport and entertainment.

The hatchling around my neck purrs in my ear, nuzzling my cheek. I cannot save it from its fate, no matter how much I try.

"I'm sorry," I press a kiss to its soft head. *"I'm so sorry."*

"Friend!" It trills. *"My friend!"*

"Yes, you are my friend," I say, before taking a deep breath and pulling away from myself. The emotions disappear. All that is left is the Beast.

I walk across the room and push open the double doors, laying my eyes upon the Candidates.

Gods. Look at them. Skinny, half-starved. Eyes full of fear. The cruelty of The Gauntlet will never cease to surprise me.

I circle them, accessing their strengths and weaknesses. Beneath my gaze, they tremble. The air turns pungent with the tangy scent of their fear and sweat.

These are not soldiers.

Something catches my eye, nearly stopping me in my tracks.

Blue eyes. No...*ice* blue. So cold, I nearly shiver. So pale, they're nearly gray. Only the slightest amount of pigment marks them as blue. The owner of the eyes stares at me, not an ounce of fear within them.

Being under the weight of her gaze feels like being struck by lightning. Her hair is tangled, but it's the strangest color. Gray, but not like the way mortal hair turns gray with age...this is different. Darker, even. Almost like ash.

The girl crosses her arms, not backing down. I don't *mean* to growl, but the noise rattles my chest. My *Beast* is reacting.

It's been ages since I could feel a reaction from it. But the girl...her eyes pull me closer. I almost step forward, close enough to touch her pale cheek, when someone coughs nearby, shocking me out of whatever hypnosis I'm in.

A Wytch. She has to be. This must be some spell. But the Fae are not stupid—not *that* stupid, at least. If they chose her, then they think she's a human. Which means whatever her real power is, it's well hidden. I continue walking around the circle, all the while accessing her scent. I caught it in the air; bitter pomegranate, burnt flowers, and fresh air.

Her magyk is old, then. Very old. I can feel her watching me, accessing me the way I had accessed her.

Who are you?

I don't know why I care but I do. Then...I remember what happened the last time I cared for someone. As my mouth opens and I drone on with the same old speech I always give, something tickles the back of my mind.

The hatchling...its magic is reaching for her. The little creature squeaks and yawns, burrowing into my hair. Several people in the crowd gasp in awe. I watch the girl's reaction carefully. She's surprised, but she hides it well.

I feel the hatchling try to speak in her mind. Feel the way it's pleased when she responds back.

But that kind of magyk is long dead...

She's not Arkaydian. They're all long dead.

It's just a coincidence.

You know there's no such thing as a coincidence, the voice of my subconscious whispers and I ignore it, suffocating it like the rest of my feelings.

Numbness is an empty, lonely place. Everything is stunted, including joy. And a small piece of me desperately wants to hold it, care for it forever, and protect it with all my might. The connection with the hatchling drops and I feel its sadness.

"I'm still here, friend," I whisper to it, all the while taking its grief within myself and suffocating that too. I am used to the pain.

This little one is not. It deserves happiness; it deserves more than this.

I survey the candidates again, pretending not to linger on the girl with ice blue eyes. I feel her presence, though. *Intimately.*

"For better or worse, you're here to compete in the Gauntlet," I tell them. "Over the next five weeks, your body is going to go through hell." I do not shout my words; I don't have to. My Beast ensures that they all hear me clearly.

"Well, that's encouraging," the girl's friend murmurs.

"If I put all of you into the Gauntlet now, none of you would make it through round one, and I'd get to watch as your bodies are fed to the Dragons. Isn't that right, little one?" I look down at the hatchling around my neck. "It's my job to prepare you to turn your sorry souls into worthwhile soldiers who will put on a damn good show. My name is Os, Gauntlet head trainer and your worst fucking nightmare."

"You took it too far, Ireyna!"

I keep replaying that moment in my head. Amalia's face cracking as her bones shattered beneath Ireyna's fist.

That's her name. *Amalia.*

I almost killed Ireyna. I imagined it; biting her neck off and tossing her head into the moat.

"You know better than to let some snide comment shatter your control!" I snarl, getting in Ireyna's face. Once, many years ago, we were lovers. It was brief and emotionless. I do not miss it; though Ireyna makes it clear that she *does.* The flirting is getting on my nerves. But this violent outburst has severed any love we once shared.

"Since when do you care?" She rolls her eyes at me. "Don't tell me you're getting soft for a little puggō? You know better, Os! They're doomed for Limbo."

I raise my hand, "Cut that sacrilegious bullshit, Rey. Why did you let her get under your skin so much? Why her?"

Ireyna crosses her arms. "Shouldn't I be asking you that since you're here?"

"Answer the question," I snap, my patience fraying as I glance at Amalia prone in the bed behind us.

I hear her bones crack again and my anger resurfaces.

Ireyna lets out a harsh breath, "She reminds me of that stupid story of the Gray Wytch. I look at her and I see my childhood nightmares, gray hair and all."

"Your past doesn't mean you get to nearly kill one of the candidates, Ireyna! Our job here is to train them and get them ready, not take them out of the game before it even takes place!" I want to rip out of this mortal skin and roar my rage at the sky. Instead, I grab the nearest vase and hurl it against the wall.

"Hurt her or any of them again and you're out," I pant, not breaking eye contact. "Do you hear me?"

Ireyna says nothing.

I'm in her face the next second.

"I said," I breathe. "Do you *hear* me?"

"Fine," she hisses, glaring up at me. "I hear you."

"Good, now get the hell out."

Ireyna bares her teeth at me as she stomps out of the room, leaving me alone with the woman who has taken up my every waking thought since laying eyes upon her.

I wait within the comfort of the shadows as her friend Dyana returns. She pulls up a chair next to Amalia's bed, and sits down, content to wait as long as needed.

It doesn't take long. I can feel Amalia's heartbeat quicken and her scent change as wakefulness returns. I can also smell Dyana's anger, mixed with hot relief.

I watch as the two argue, but Dyana's words stop me.

"No, you don't get to do that," her voice gets louder, and the younger woman stands up. "You're not going to belittle how godsdamned traumatic it was seeing you get nearly beaten to death. And you just expected me to stand there, silent. I thought you were going to die, Amalia!"

Amalia stretches her jaw before sighing and pulling Dyana down next to her. She resists for a moment before finally acquiescing.

"You're right," she says quietly, as if the words are difficult to say. "I was scared, and then Ireyna spouted her Sol Constantus bullshit, and I got angry."

"Angry enough to lose?" Dyana asks, but she's less shocked. I see understanding settling into her soul from behind her warm brown eyes.

"Angry enough to do many things; losing is merely one of them," Amalia admits.

She lost on purpose. Ireyna is no easy target. For her to lose on purpose she...*she would have to be strong. Unbelievably so.*

Dyana sighs, "I'll go tell the healers you're up, but I'm fucking mad at you, okay? You're all I have too, you know. And that means you need to protect my best friend instead of acting stupid to prove a point and get Ireyna in trouble."

Amalia's face goes blank, "I have no idea what you're talking about."

Liar. Such a little liar.

There is no sound at all—nothing besides her breathing. No obvious change in the room, but I feel the moment Amalia becomes aware of my presence.

I watch her from the shadows, listening as her heart begins to race. Stepping out of the shadows, I lean against the doorframe to the room. We just stare at each other, and after a few moments and I let my magyk flare. Not visibly, but in a way that if she is who I think she is...Amalia would notice it.

Her eyes widen just a smidge. Enough to tell me she did see it.

"You're lucky, waking up before the Welcome ball. If you missed it, they would have killed you," I say casually, holding my Beast back with every breath.

"Such kind hosts, your friends." Amalia gives me an annoyed smile.

I push away from the door and move faster than she can track. One moment I'm across the room, the next, I hover over her, my hands braced on the headboard above her bed.

It's amusing to watch as she tries not to jump. It's barely noticeable, but I hear the tiny gasp leave her pink lips.

Stop thinking about her fucking lips, Os! my self-conscious roars.

But my Beast...I hear his words too.

Claim her. Mark her. Make her ours. OURS. OURS. OURS!

It's been years since I could hear the thoughts of my other nature. I thought perhaps it was long lost. Yet now it demands her.

"It took three Fae healers to fix your face," I murmur, tracing the planes of her angular face with my eyes. "They had to break some of your other bones and part of your left femur, using it to mold a new jaw. Then they had to regrow that bone too, which is why you now have a little purple scar on your left thigh."

My words do not affect her. She meets my gaze, refusing to show any emotion.

I fight a smile at the display of stubbornness. It's rather draconian of her.

"They did a shit job. It still hurts," Amalia says, raising a brow.

"It will. All magyk has limits, and they healed you the best they could. The swelling will go down in a few days."

"You speak from experience."

"Yes." I force the word out. I didn't even mean to be that honest, but Amalia Roth disarms me in a way I do not yet understand.

"Your teammate is surprisingly strong. I thought she was going to try and wrestle me to the ground when I went to carry you to the healers."

I expect her to smile. It's very clear that she loves her friend dearly.

"All you Magyka think humans are so weak when in reality, you're just jealous that they feel more, what with the short life span."

"Finished preaching, then?" I ask.

What are you?

"Not preaching, just the truth. You think Dyana and I are weak. I just don't like bigoted Magyka who think they're better than everyone else."

"You're angry." I note. Unable to help myself, I lean down slightly, catching her scent in the air. The sound of her heart *thumps* in my ears.

"Yes, of course I'm angry!" She hisses the words and scoots away from me. "Fae and the other races treat humans like vermin. As if we're dirty. Well, you know what, we are because you and your fucking overlords don't allow enough food to be traded, so we're all starving. Yes, I'm angry, and you will never understand that."

I feel it. The moment something hidden deep within the tethers that lock me in this form *snap*. Just a single thread in the rope. But it snaps and my eyes *shift*.

Amalia's eyes widen.

"You've made up your mind about me quickly." My is voice deeper, richer, smokier. My Beast is so close to the surface. "But you're right. Most Magyka and Fae here think of humans as animals, so you'd be wise to watch that pretty mouth of yours and be careful not to talk like that when wandering ears could be listening. Say any of that to one of the Fae, and your head will be added to the pile of skulls decorating the Arena while they watch as the Dragons feast on your scrawny flesh."

"Yes, I'll keep my mouth shut so you can train us to die for them. What a great plan," she snaps back, but I can smell her fear. Along with a hint of something else, something warmer, spicier, like my flames but not. Almost as if she...

She wants ussssss, my Beast hisses.

Amalia suddenly leans back and slaps herself across the face. I take a step back, alarmed.

"Had a little itch in my jaw," she says with a casual shrug. She's...trying to throw me off.

I can see through your game, little liar. While she focuses on trying to drive me to anger, my eyes can't help but watch her lips. So pink...so soft.

Soft things in a harsh world are to be cherished.

Protected.

PROTECT HER! my Beast screams at me.

Her scent grows warmer, spicier.

She *likes* that I'm watching her.

"Tell me something, Amalia Roth," I let my eyes travel down her delicious body, taking it in from beneath the flimsy white nightgown.

I lean down until our noses nearly touch.

The new scars along her jaw only enhance her beauty. They sharpen it; for she is a blade.

"Tell me why you planned to lose."

Amalia's pupils go wide.

"I lost on purpose because Ireyna is a racist bitch, and I didn't want her to retaliate if I fought for real. She seemed to be waiting for an excuse to hurt me."

Mostly true.

"You weren't trying, though, even after the first major injury," I remind her.

"You're right. I'm more out of shape than I let on, and it was hard to think through the pain." She shrugs, saying the words automatically. She's told this story many times, then.

"I was unaware you were monitoring my fight that closely. Perhaps you just like seeing women get beat up?" she asks, a smirk playing on her face.

Trying to find my buttons? I see through you, little liar.

"Don't; it won't work." I brush off her attempt.

"What do you mean?" she asks innocently.

"This little game. You're trying to push my buttons to elicit a response. But I'll warn you; it won't work." I flash my fangs, leaning into that fraying string on the cage that imprisons me.

I blame my beast rising to the surface for the way I lean down and drag my nose up Amalia's soft little neck. Her pale skin is freckled after years in the sun. Moles and other scars decorate her arms.

I suddenly find myself wanting to map each freckle with my tongue.

"If you bite me, little liar, you'll find I bite back," I whisper to her, leaning back. Her pupils go wide again and this time, when her heart begins to race, I can *feel* that it's from the lust swirling in her being.

Amalia Roth *wants* me.

"Be careful, Amalia Roth," I warn. "I'll destroy you and leave nothing left. How terrible it would be to deprive the Fae of another glorious death."

The latter words are automatic, because the mere thought of her death makes me want to rip the arena to shreds, stone by fucking stone.

"I apologize." You could cut her sarcasm with a knife.

My hand raises, my fingers caressing her jaw, tracing the new scars. Amalia doesn't look away. Those ice blue eyes never leave mine. But she's not afraid.

Not truly.

Her pink, pillowy lips call to me. I rub my thumb over them and feel her tongue dart out, tasting me.

"Interesting," I breathe, before using all my remaining strength to force my body to stand and walk away, leaving Amalia alone.

CHAPTER 19
NYALL

I fucking hate balls. They're a waste of time and a waste of money. But Father loves to put on a show, and putting on a show means playing the part.

It's all a hollow, carved out *lie*—me included.

Tolys enters with the first of the Candidates, distracting me from my thoughts. I listen as they drone on with endless names of different cities. It's the same song and dance every 25 fucking years. The same bloodshed for *nothing*.

My interest piques as Sud Azyl is called, though I don't show it. I force my face to remain still as Mirielle walks in, resplendent in dark green.

She looks so human. That's why this works. Whether the rest of this will work is…quite questionable, not that I let any of the rebels know that. They need me to be strong, not doubting.

Mirielle joins the crowd and I brush against her magyk, letting her know I'm here.

"You good?" My words flow into her thoughts.

"Fine. These shoes fucking hurt though," she groans.

I snicker. *"Woe is you. At least you don't have to sit next to my Father all night and actually laugh at his rude jokes."*

"Suddenly the pain is bearable," Mirielle jokes. *"You sure this whole thing is going to work?"*

"Win the Gauntlet, then we'll work on the rest."

"No pressure," Mirielle sighs. I leave her mind and come back to myself.

Twyn Fells is next. The northernmost town in the kingdom. The candidates from the Fells are always weak and skinny, more so than the rest. Food is scarce up there, thanks to the temperature.

"DYANA ARKOS!" Tolys calls. I watch as a tall, dark haired woman walks in. She's so young. Only 24, 25 at most. The blue silk dress hugs her lean figure. Her warm brown eyes look around with a hesitant confidence. But Dyana lifts her chin and walks confidently towards the stage. I'm behind the High Council, hidden out of the spotlight.

"AMALIA ROTH!"

I look to the top of the stairs and all of the breath leaves my lungs.

Who is that?

Ice blue eyes, so pale, so cold, watch the crowd with the assessment of a predator. Black kohl lines them, only emphasizing their piercing depth. Long, ash gray hair streams down her back in waves as the woman begins the long walk down the staircase.

Her dress, if you could call it that, is so thin, it's nearly transparent. The shadows of her legs play against gleaming silk the color of steel. Every step reveals a high slit, showing her delicious, creamy thighs.

I've always found women beautiful. I enjoy all creatures. But the *desire* that stirs within me at the sight of her body...that is rare. She wears a metal shoulder piece made of black chainmail.

My eyes travel back up to her face which is when I pause. I know that look. She's...angry. No, not angry, she's *furious.*

Amalia Roth stares at the High Council with murder in her gaze. It's not perfectly apparent, but she doesn't hide it either.

She looks at my father like she's seen a ghost. She looks at him the way *I* look at him.

Amalia Roth.

Amalia Roth.

I repeat the name over and over again in my head, memorizing it, tasting each letter.

"Welcome to Castael Laryn—" My father stands, addressing the group, but I do not watch the Candidates. I watch her.

"—and welcome to the 25th Gauntlet! Every Gauntlet we remember the brave Fae souls who lost their lives in the Uprising and remember the misguided ways of the vicious, evil humans who thought themselves higher than the mighty Fae.

"All of you undoubtedly will die, except for the lucky human left standing!" One of the other high councilors whispers, and the Father rolls his eyes, "Or two of you, should someone get disqualified." He says the word as if it's poison in his mouth, puckering his lips in distaste. "Let me make this perfectly clear now; should any of you think of using disqualification as a way to take the easy way out, don't. If any of you are found to be faking injuries at any point in time, the punishments will be severe." The crowd snickers as our group shuffles awkwardly. Father continues, "This Gauntlet is the hardest one we've ever had. I think many of you," he looks to the crowd of sycophantic Fae, "will be pleasantly surprised with what we have in store.

"But after hearing whispers of so many humans kidnapping innocent Demis all around the country, I've decided perhaps we've been too generous, too gentle. After taking solace and conferring with our Lord, Constantyn, He sent a vision, showing me the path forward. The prize for this Gauntlet is hereby decreased to 50,000 gold marks. I don't like to be mean,"—the other High Councilors all look sad, as if this was a difficult decision for them— "but I will not feed this nasty, sinful rumor mill further. Perhaps if the humans and Magyka decide to behave by the next Gauntlet, we will reconsider. But it seems you need to be reminded of your place again." The crowd laughs as Father sits down.

I look around at the crowd, and molten gold eyes meet mine—*Os.*

He's in fine black armor over pristine black fighting leathers, his shoulder-length hair pulled back, making his eyes even sharper. He looks dangerous, but he just stares at me, unblinking.

I watch as his gaze moves from me, and onto Amalia Roth. But her gaze isn't on him.

Her gaze is on *me.*

It takes her a moment to realize I'm watching her as she checks me out. The feeling of her eyes tracing my body makes all the blood rush to my cock.

So, I wink at her.

Amalia blushes and looks away.

"Now, this is a momentous occasion, so let us celebrate!" Father calls, lifting both hands in the air just slightly, signaling something.

I don't know Father's plans for the night...but the second I see our Fae attendants walk in dressed in long white robes, each of them carrying small, wiggling bundles...I know.

I don't watch as the young Dragons wiggle, screaming in fear as Councilor Varas pulls out a knife. I don't watch as the other High Councilors do the same.

I only watch her. Even as blood sprays and screams ring out, as the High Council consumes the young Dragons.

I watch as Amalia Roth *breaks.*

CHAPTER 20
OS

Someday, I will kill them. All of them. And when I do, I'm going to make it *hurt*.

Every year, I feel my sanity fade. With every death, the part of me that *loves* diminishes.

In another five centuries, there will be nothing left. I will be no better than the Dragonguard.

A husk. A shell of a Dragon and empty on the inside.

Only the truly evil would hurt a child, a youngling. I wish I was surprised that this is how the night ended, but there is nothing they can do to surprise me. No low they won't stoop to. So, I'm not surprised they would do this, that they would be this cruel.

I know all about the depths of the High Council's cruelty.

What I am *very* surprised about is the fact that Amalia Roth just took the pain away from the hatchlings.

Which means she's Arkaydian. An Arkaydian, right under their noses. How the hell she's managed to stay alive, I'm not sure. But I *feel* it in her magyk. I can also feel her panic. Her little heart is racing so hard I'm half sure it might jump right out of her chest.

Her eyes are wide and her face, bloodless.

That panic...I understand it. Sweet Livyathin, do I understand it.

It's how I felt the first time I watched them slaughter hatchlings alive.

But I also know that if Amalia Roth is an Arkaydian, none of us can afford for her to lose control.

She's a loose cannon.

The second the blades began to slice across the hatchling's throats, I'm by Amalia's side. A strangled sound leaves her mouth as the air turns both hot and cold, signaling the nearing storm.

I wrap my arm around her waist. Amalia is in such a state of despair and shock that she lets me. Her dress is so thin, I can feel the curves of her body. I lead her out of the room, pulling her along easily.

Amalia's pupils are dilated and her face bloodless.

"They killed them," she whispers, her voice trembling with mania. "They killed them all."

"Amalia? Amalia!" her friend cries, following behind us as I pull Amalia to the edge of the room.

"I've got her," I whisper to her Dyana—her friend and teammate—who watches me with a fair amount of suspicion. "I'll get her out of here. I...panic too."

I don't think Amalia hears me, because she doesn't react. But her friend Dyana blinks in surprise before nodding.

"Hurt her and I'll gut you," Dyana whispers, glaring at me.

Is this human trying to scare me? How cute.

Clearly she's taken after Amalia.

Dyana grabs the hand of her redhaired friend—the candidate from Sud Azyl. Mirielle, I think. I pull on Amalia's arm and get her out of the ballroom. Even at the edge of the room, we have to weave through the thick crowd and tables of food until we reach the doors.

"They killed them," Amalia says, her voice hysterical. I can feel her magyk aching to be let out.

That *cannot* happen.

"Calm yourself," I gently ease into her mind, not wanting to scare her.

"Leave me alone," she gasps, voice shaky.

"I will not. Now, breathe." I force the command out, and her body responds.

Not a compulsion, simply an order from a predator. It is in their nature to listen.

"Again." I force her lungs to inflate with air. Silent sobs still wreck her.

"How the hell is he able to communicate with me like this?" The thought isn't meant for me, but I hear it anyways. Her walls are non-existent.

We make our way out of the Citadel and emerge into the gardens.

"Get out of my fucking head," Amalia snarls, shoving at me frantically. I see the moment she realizes the blood of the hatchlings now coats her face. She lifts a hand, touching the droplets, and examines her red fingers.

With a strangled sound, she falls to the ground and empties her stomach.

"Leave me alone," she groans, wiping her mouth with the back of her hand.

"No," I say.

"I said, leave me the fuck alone!"

I want to smile.

She's full of such *fire.*

"And I said no. You're a flight risk."

"Oh, get off your godsdamn high horse. We're all flight risks, you overgrown herring." She pushes herself to standing and shoves my chest, "Now leave!"

But I see it. That glimmer of *shame.*

"You don't want me to see you upset," I realize. "That's why you're getting angry. You're embarrassed?"

She gasps, "Are you reading my emotions?"

"Yes." No reason to lie to her.

I watch as the panic suddenly overwhelms her, clasping her tightly within its grasp.

"I need, I need to get this off," she mumbles frantically.

"What are you talking about?

"Get it off. Get the blood off. I need—I need to get it off. Get it the FUCK OFF." She begins screaming and tearing at her dress as if it's suffocating her.

"Calm yourself," I try and soothe, but it doesn't work. With my magyk I brush against her mind, but the panic magnifies tenfold within her thoughts.

*"Get it off, get it off, **GET IT OFF!"*** A reedy whine falls from her lips.

"You have to calm down," I warn. I can feel her magyk. The scent gets stronger, and her skin begins to warm.

I don't know why or how, but I just know I cannot let her lose control.

"Can't." She pants, terror in her voice. She looks around and suddenly sprints towards a large fountain in the middle of the garden.

"What the fuck are you doing?" I call, but Amalia leaps, jumping straight in the water.

"Godsdamnit," I groan before tracing over to the fountain and reaching beneath the surface, grabbing hold of her, and hauling Amalia onto the ground.

She's soaking wet and panting, but I see the panic leaving her eyes.

Before she can say a word, I'm picking her up and tossing her over my shoulder.

We need to get out of sight.

"If you don't put me down, I swear to Gods I will rip out your godsdamn throat, you hulking bear!" she screams at me as her fists begin pummeling my back.

YES. OURS. SHE IS OURS. CLAIM HER. MATE HER. PROTECT HER. The voice of my Beast is so close to the surface, I feel its talons dragging across my human skin, desperate to break out.

"Be quiet," I snarl, but she continues shouting and slapping me.

It's my Beast who emerges as I let out a snarl and spank Amalia on her pert little ass.

"Did you just slap my ass?" she shrieks. "I'm going to fucking KILL YOU!"

"Be quiet. Or you'll get us both in trouble if any soldiers catch us. You think they need any more excuses or reasons to beat any of us bloody?" At that, she quiets down. We enter the Dragon Pit and descend the staircase, not to the Pit itself but to the living quarters. Instead of taking her back to her dormitory, I take a left, going to the wing where my room is located.

"Wrong turn?" she asks, her voice gravely.

"I don't trust you to be alone right now."

I push open the doors to my room and let out a breath I didn't realize I was holding.

"Put me down." Her voice is empty and ragged. I gently let her down, making sure she doesn't fall, but Amalia just slaps my hands away.

"What is this?" Amalia gestures stiffly to the room.

"My quarters."

"Okay, well I'm going back to my rooms." She turns, pushing past me to leave but I catch her arm.

"Not looking like that, you aren't," I growl.

I've been trying to keep my eyes off her body but now that she stands here before me...

The breath is stolen right out of my lungs, would that I call her the thief.

She's resplendent. The glow from my fireplace plays off her skin, creating shadows along the edge of her body and leaving nothing to the imagination.

OURS. OURS. OURS. OURS. My Beast roars to the heavens. I want to let my head fall back and scream it alongside him.

I want to do many, many things, most of which involve Amalia Roth naked and at my mercy.

"Sit down; you're wearing a hole in my rug," I murmur before disappearing into the safety of my closet. I take a deep breath and brace my hands on the upper shelf.

Staying in control is a struggle. Need for Amalia Roth burns in my blood.

I emerge from the closet and hand Amalia a spare top and pair of pants.

"Turn around. I need to change." She motions with her finger, but I don't move.

"Ah, I forgot humans are such prudes," I say, watching the frustration build on her face.

The *challenge.*

She stares me down but I just wait.

I am a Dragon; I have endless patience. With a snarl worthy of a Dragon, Amalia begins trying to untangle herself from her dress.

She doesn't get far. The wet fabric mixed with her long, wet hair and the metal armor means she quickly ends up getting stuck. Amalia lets out a frustrated whimper.

"Need some assistance?" I ask, and she looks up to meet my gaze. I let the hunger I feel flare within my eyes.

"Actually yes, I do. I think I'm stuck," she says begrudgingly. I'm at Amalia's back a second later.

"Don't move. You'll make it worse," I order. Amalia gasps at my touch as her body leans into me instinctively. Her hips sway backward slightly and I feel the way she tenses, fighting her own need.

I gently untangle her hair from the armor before trying to lift it off, but it gets stuck.

"Fucking imperial Fae designs..." I mutter. Frustration wins and I rip the fabric with a snarl. Free from the shoulder piece, I finish untangling Amalia's hair, brushing through it with my fingers.

"So unusual. Like liquid smoke," I mutter as the silky strands glide across my hand.

Amalia snorts but there is no humor in it. "Unusual; that's a new one. I'll add that to the list alongside 'ugly' and 'scary'."

"Humans fear what they don't understand."

She *hums* in agreement. Her hair feels so nice, I don't want to stop touching it.

Ever.

I raise my hands and bury my fingers in her scalp, massaging lightly. Amalia lets out a low groan and leans back into me fully.

A wave of her sent hits me. Spicy, bitter pomegranate.

"Your scent is very strange," I whisper.

She glares at me over her shoulder, her ice blue eyes relaxed and sleepy, "Wow, just what every woman wants to hear."

Her face is painted in firelight. I am no painter or artist, but I suddenly understand why some feel compelled to memorialize an image. I could look at Amalia all night.

"Humans usually have a very particular scent."

"And you, Amalia Roth, you don't smell like a human," I enter her mind and brush my magyk against hers. *"You smell like home."*

She turns more fully, facing me. "I smell like home?"

My heart breaks at the confusion in her voice.

"Yes. Your scent reminds me of home," I nod. "I enjoy it."

Her mouth opens in shock before she closes it, catching herself. "Thanks."

I turn Amalia and get back to my untangling, but the air is tense.

"I don't know why I would smell like that since I'm not from here. I've never left the North until now. So, it must be from being near so many Fae tonight," she rambles.

Amalia is *nervous.* How adorable.

"Perhaps," finished with her hair, I turn Amalia, facing her once more. "But there is much you don't know, little liar."

At my words, Amalia gasps.

I step towards her, and she steps back. We enter a dance as I prowl closer and closer until eventually, her back hits the wall near the fireplace. I slide my leg between hers and grab her chin, tilting it gently until she's looking up into my eyes.

Gods.

I was going to say something but having her caught between my body and the wall is addling my thoughts.

Her scent fills the air, hypnotizing me. Leaning down, I nearly brush my lips against hers, but not quite. Instead, I hover just before her, so close she can feel my breath.

PLAY. The thought hits me instantly. My Beast wants to toy with her. It's one of the ways Dragons typically show affection.

So as Amalia leans forward to kiss me, I pull back and smirk, "Get changed before you catch a cold."

She blinks, and I'm gone. Back in the chair a meter away as I watch her process. Her eyes go wide before narrowing at me in fury.

There it is. There's the *fire.*

If I didn't know better, I would swear Amalia Roth was a Dragon. A creature, at least. Her ice blue eyes sparkle with anger, but I don't miss the hint of pleasure.

She wants to play too.

Amalia smirks and slowly pushes the sleeves of her dress down one by one.

My heart stops as she teases the edge of the fabric and slowly expose her pert, perfect breasts in full. I nearly groan aloud at the sight of her pink nipples, hard and begging for my mouth. The arms of the chair creak loudly beneath my tight grip as my control is shredded by the perfect creature in front of me.

But Amalia doesn't stop there. She continues peeling off the dress, pushing it past her hips with a torturously slow pace.

All thought empties from my brain as her nude figure is revealed.

The dress hits the floor.

I'm in such shock, I can't even move as Amalia bends down, grabs the dress, and throws it at my face. The fabric is heavy and it slaps me across the nose, knocking me back slightly.

"Oh, what *terrible* human aim I have," she croons before walking over to me and—Gods, help me—bending over to grab the dress.

My growl shakes the walls as I take in her round, delicious ass.

Too soon, Amalia's figure is covered, though the shirt is still sheer.

"Did you pick this on purpose?" she asks, eyes narrowed with suspicion.

I smirk, "*So* sorry."

"Fuck you," she snarls.

"There she is," I meet her snarl with one of my own. "That's the real you, not this fake, fearful, rule-abiding mask you put on."

"Why did you get me out of there? Me losing my shit doesn't mean anything to you. My life is inconsequential. So why do something about it? And on that note, how can you speak to me mentally?"

How masterful she is at changing the topic.

I nod. "How about this? I'll answer some of your questions, little liar," she bares her teeth at that nickname, "if you tell me why an Arkaydian pretending to be human is competing in the Gauntlet."

I watch as it hits her.

That I know her little secret.

"I have no idea what you're talking about," Amalia's face is as cold as her eyes. "But I do know that suggesting an Arkaydian still lives, let alone in Ur Daoine, is treason."

"It is indeed treason," I watch her, "but I *felt* you, Amalia Roth. I felt you die with them."

She flinches as if I struck her.

"You're delusional," she scoffs, denying the truth. "You felt nothing; you only saw someone shocked and disgusted at a heinous act."

I don't disagree.

Amalia's eyes turn fierce as her words sharpen. "When they emerged with the hatchlings, what did you do, exactly? Ah," she snaps her fingers, "that's right. You did *nothing*. So, let's not point fingers just because I have feelings."

She might as well take her dagger out and stab me in the chest.

That would hurt less than the truth in her words.

The fight in me dies a little as sadness takes over. "I'm not going to turn you in, Amalia. I realize you think I support the Fae but let me be perfectly clear. I do not support the Fae in any way, shape, or form, and you're right; what happened tonight was horrific and a perversion of nature. I curse the Gods every night for not unleashing the full weight of their fury upon the High Council's heads for their actions against Dragons."

Amalia watches me, the fight still in her eyes, "So you say."

"What I said is true; all of it. I'm not going to turn you in," I nod. "But you do need training or you're going to get yourself, and your friends, killed."

"Trust with a caveat, right?" Amalia scoffs. "You'll only keep this secret if I submit to your demands. It's comforting, how predictable you are. As if you really expect me to trust you."

My anger returns in an instant, burning so brightly I'm surprised steam doesn't rise off my skin. *"Get one thing into your pretty little head; I am not Fae."* I snarl in Amalia's mind. *"Best you learn that now because I'm the only one who can teach you about your magyk."*

"Then why do you want to teach me illegal magyk, and how the hell do you know how to do it in the first place?" she asks, and I feel her genuine confusion.

This is going to be tricky.

"A few types of beings in Ur Daoine have the gift of empathy," I say carefully.

"I'm not an empath," Amalia protests. *"I can only work magyk with animals."*

"That's because you weren't taught correctly."

Based on her reaction, I'm correct.

"How about we make a deal?" I say aloud. "I promise to keep your secret if you promise to keep my...lack of certain allegiances to yourself. Deal?"

I see the moment Amalia caves, "Fine. But let's just agree that it's clear you're clearly upper Magyka. I won't pry more than that, but that much I do know."

"I'm upper Magyka, but I am not Fae. For now, that is all I can give you."

True. *True.*

She nods, pleased at least with that slight admission.

Unable to help myself, I reach up and touch her drying hair.

"Is this a part of the deal?" she whispers.

I want to smile at the way her voice trembles.

Fuck it. In one swift motion, I stand and wrap her in my arms, putting my thigh between her legs and *pulsing* against her clit. The gasp she lets out is music to my ears. Instantly, I want more. I need to hear her make that sound again.

"Is what part of the deal, little liar?" I drag my nose up her delicate neck.

Her scent suddenly gets spicier, *muskier.*

Amalia wants me. Wants this.

Pride washes through me.

She wants me.

She wants me.

Unable to recall the last time this happened, I lean back, meet her gaze, and smile.

Her mouth opens and her eyes go wide in shock at the sight.

"You know..." I lick my lips. "I feel like we can kill two birds with one stone. Let me show you just how much you can trust me. Let me take care of that needy cunt, Amalia."

Fuck. I'm trying not to scare her but with every second she rubs herself against me, my control gets thinner and thinner.

"Do you permit?" I hiss the word, my Beast so close to the surface I can *almost* feel the shift. I rock my leg into her once more, grinding into her. I can feel her wetness soaking into my pants.

"Oh gods, oh gods, oh gods." The thought isn't for me, but I respond anyways.

"When I taste you, it won't be the Gods you cry out for, little liar."

Amalia's mouth opens wider as she grabs hold of me, grinding into my leg.

"Do you permit?" I whisper, devouring her moans.

"I—"

BANG, BANG, BANG. I'm about to respond when someone knocks on the door so hard it rattles.

Godsdamnit.

Water from the waterspout in my bathroom pours over my head.

I can't get Amalia out of my head.

I close my eyes and all I see are hers; icy and cold, yet burning with such fury, such passion, it robs me of my breath.

Her naked body plays on repeat in my thoughts, stealing away my ability to function.

My cock is still throbbing and my balls ache. I've been hard ever since I saw her body beneath that wet dress.

Reaching down, I grab a bar of soap and create a rich lather before reaching down and fisting myself.

It's been a while since I've felt like this, but all it takes is closing my eyes to imagine it's Amalia's pale hands around my cock.

I stroke myself with one hand while tugging on my heavy sack with the other, imaging it's her, kneeling at my feet.

That's all it takes.

With a roar, I come hard, coating my hands in my own pleasure. It keeps going so long, I nearly stumble.

Panting, I finish rinsing off, but the ache, the *need*—it doesn't go away. It grows *stronger*.

CHAPTER 21
NYALL

"So, what *is* the plan exactly?" Mirielle asks. It's almost morning, but I barely notice. I don't sleep much these days.

"I'm working on it," I sigh. "Right now, we just need you to get to the finals. From there..."

"You'll what, just *stab* your Father?" Mirielle asks, her brows raised in disbelief. "Because nobody's tried *that* before."

Cheeky shit.

"I said I'm working on it. I need to make a connection with the Dragons, but they won't speak to me."

Mirielle watches me carefully. "Have you ever spoken with Os?"

At the mention of his name, my blood goes cold.

"Yes, I have. He will be no help here."

"I thought you said you were friends, once."

"We were, *once*. But that time is long past."

"I see. Well, then we'll have to figure something else out."

I walk over to her and put my arm around her shoulders. We've known each other for centuries. Once, Mirielle was someone I considered a friend. Now I consider her family.

"I'll get you out if anything happens, okay?" I reassure her.

She rolls her pale green eyes, but I feel the way her body relaxes slightly. "Someone has to get you out too, you know."

I smirk. "Of course. The world simply wouldn't survive without my pretty face."

Mirielle's answering snort makes me smile.

"For now, continue to lay low and integrate with the other Candidates. You're doing a great job pairing up with the Northerners. This isn't something you should go through alone."

"I'm fine," Mirielle rolls her eyes before her face turns stony. "I didn't plan on joining their little friendship, but...it's nice. They're nice. Although the one with the gray hair—Amalia—she's a bit rough around the edges."

I nod, but my mind goes elsewhere. Amalia Roth. The woman in silver. The Candidate from Twyn Fells. As Mirielle finishes giving me her update and we part ways, I find myself lost in my own thoughts.

The suns are already rising. There's no reason to try and go to sleep now. Instead, I use a spell to shift my clothes, changing into something suitable for sitting in a saddle.

I need to clear my head.

Already, I can feel the tension easing out of my body.

The rhythmic clomping of Aanad's hooves is always comforting. Her shiny black coat glimmers in the morning light. As she glances back at me, the faintest outline of a shiny red horn appears. It's not always visible. Part of me wonders if she can control when it appears.

As Aanad walks through the city gates click softly and squeeze my calves, urging her into a trot. She whinnies happily and obliges, prancing forward eagerly as she chomps on her bit. Some horses enjoy riding without a bit, but since Aanad has such sharp fangs, I've found she enjoys taking some of her aggression out on the piece of metal.

Better that than chunks of flesh from anyone standing near us.

When she makes it closer to the safety of the Annag, a dense forest around the city's southwestern edge that spans across the Abhaynn Gheal, I give her the reins and let her stretch her legs as we break into a fast canter.

Breathe.

Big, gulping, cleansing breaths relax the tightness in my chest as worry drains from me.

Breathe.

My arms fall to my side as Aanad slows into a rocking canter as we trace the outskirts of the forest.

Breathe.

A sound in the distance catches my attention and I glance up to see the backside of a large, white horse with a black tail.

Then I see the gray hair, flying in the wind.

Amalia.

I whistle to Aanad who increases her speed. The Oryx can go much faster than this if she wished, but I just want to catch up to the rider in front of us.

Aanad catches sight of the white horse and lets out a piercing shriek.

I roll my eyes and laugh.

Oryx mares only make noises like that when they see a male horse they like.

Aanad thinks the white horse is *cute.*

As I get closer to Amalia and her horse, magyk brushes against my mind. Suddenly the white horse darts forward, much faster than it should be able to move. Aanad lets out another shriek of happiness as she chases him down and it lets out another shriek. Much to my surprise, the white horse neighs back, clearly asking Aanad to play.

We race down the forest's edge so fast that it almost feels like we're flying. Mud flies as Aanad's hooves hit the ground heavily. The forest narrows as we approach the Abhaynn Gheal.

I slow as soon as I see the large tree blocking the path. Rot covers the thick trunk, completely blocking the path. Expecting Amalia to do the same, her eyes meet mine as she lets out a loud laugh and pushes her horse forward.

Fuck. She's going to jump it.

The shock at seeing her smile renders me useless. All I can do is watch as the white horse takes a giant leap, crossing the log. Aanad lets out another shriek and races forward, nearly unseating me with the movement. I gather my seat, sinking my weight into my tailbone and down my legs as the red horn on Aanad's forehead becomes clearer.

She charges the log with an excited whinny, lowering her head and piercing it with her sharp horn. The log explodes, sending shards everywhere. As we emerge through the destruction, I'm met with Amalia Roth's shocked face.

"I'm surprised a horse that size could make the jump," I laugh.

"How the hell do you have an Oryx?" she asks, her eyes roving over Aanad.

We pull up next to the slightly overweight white horse, who neighs and smacks Aanad with his tail. The two creatures shift closer, before Aanad reaches around and starts nibbling lightly on the gelding's thick black mane.

"I found Aanad in the meat trade after her mother was slaughtered. She was dying, only a few days old, and on her way to slaughter, so I bought her and nursed her back to health. She's been by my side ever since, the spoiled little brat." I meet Amalia's icy blue eyes as I run my hand along Aanad's neck.

"Well deserved spoiling, it sounds like," she murmurs. Aanad raises her head from the white horse's neck, gently sniffing Amalia's palm.

"You're beautiful," she whispers, scratching her velvet cheek.

"Oh good, just what she needs. A bigger ego." I tease, and Amalia smiles back.

Fuck.

She's stunning. Suddenly overheated, I take off my hat and run my hand through my hair.

"Why were you following me?" Amalia asks plainly, her smile falling.

"I do this ride every morning. Or at least, I try to. Timing doesn't always work out. So, I believe you are following me and joining in on my ride." I smile, and Amalia narrows her eyes.

"Be that as it may, you started the race, and what were those results again? Oh, that's right, you lost. How did I forget?" Her smile is full of sarcasm this time.

We fall silent for a few seconds, watching each other.

Finally, Amalia nods. "We need to be getting back." She clicks her tongue, urging her horse forward.

I nudge Aanad who eagerly follows her new friend.

"May I escort you back to the gates?" I ask. We take the long way, walking around the log this time.

"Because surely I'm too weak to make it back myself, being human and all."

The way she says "human" makes me pause. Carefully, so carefully she wouldn't be able to tell, I brush my magyk against hers. Not enough to touch it, but enough to sense it.

No. Not human at all, then. Which means Mirielle isn't the only spy in the Gauntlet this year.

Why are you hiding your magyk? I brush my power against hers some more, testing it.

I can't tell what she is. But *God,* even being close to her power makes me *burn.* It's like touching a living flame. I half-expect to look down at my hands and see charred skin.

I pull back before she can sense me, but my curiosity is piqued.

"I never assumed you were human," I wink at her, and her eyes go wide. I immediately regret my words. "That was rude of me. I'm sorry."

"Yes, it was," she hesitates, "but I...appreciate the apology."

I get the feeling that Amalia Roth isn't the kind of person to trust another being easily, if at all. I don't want to jeopardize this moment by being a rude asshole.

The last person I apologized to this way was Os.

Amalia meets my gaze once more, her face stony and unsure. She nods, saying her goodbyes, before clicking at her horse forward. Aanad and I watch as they disappear into the distance, heading back to the city.

Aanad lets out a low rumbling whine.

"We need to play this carefully," I whisper to her, "which means letting them go." Aanad snorts and paws the ground, clearly annoyed at my answer. I reach forward and stroke her neck. before clicking my tongue and urging her into a slow, easy trot.

"I have a feeling we will see them again," I say to her. If only I had known how soon that would be...and how terribly it would go.

CHAPTER 22
NYALL

It's like drowning; having to watch an innocent creature get tortured and knowing there is nothing you can do to stop it. Not without making it so much worse.

I'm standing in a crowd, shoulder-to-shoulder with my evil prick of a Father, and there is nothing I can do but *drown* as Amalia Roth is beaten by a guard at our feet.

The sound of her face shattering beneath the guard's fist nearly rips me in two. Centuries of honing my control is destroyed in an instant.

There was no crime she committed. None other than loving her horse. The guards caught her napping, and today they decided that was unacceptable.

I was going to let her go, of course, and I'm kicking myself for not doing it sooner...before *he* showed up.

As soon as I heard them chant my Father's name, I knew this day would end in bloodshed. It always does with him.

"Enough," Father waves off the guards as Amalia slumps to the ground, her face so destroyed, it makes me want to scream. No one noticed the white glowing symbol on my palm as I wove a spell to knock her unconscious.

If Father paid any true attention to me, he would have noticed. Then it would have been my face getting shattered and my body beaten. Slowly, so slowly, I look to the side. It's physically painful to take my eyes off her, and it only causes my anger to burn brighter.

Os watches Amalia, his body trembling. The fury in his golden eyes makes my hair stand on end.

In the past, being confronted with the reality of his affections would have hurt me. But there is no hurt as I watch him watch *her*. Strangely, there is only a feeling of rightness.

There is no fiercer protector to have than Remus Ostia.

Father leaves, walking back to the Citadel, but Os runs over and grabs Amalia, hoisting her into his arms. The big male handles her with such tender gentility, it nearly brings me to tears.

I want to say something, I want to go with them, I want to tear the clouds from the fucking sky with the fountain of rage simmering within me.

Instead, I follow my Father like the dutiful, sycophant son, drowning in a sea of guilt and regret.

CHAPTER 23
NYALL

Amalia never saw me watching her.

I've spent many years sneaking in and out of the Dragon Pit, though, those memories are difficult to remember. Not because I can't remember them, but because it reminds me of...him.

But I stood there, cloaked in shadows, and I watched as Amalia Roth spoke to a Dragon. Not just any Dragon either, the legendary Crimson Queen. She *spoke* to it, and based on her reaction, the Dragon spoke back. I leave the Dragon Pit before Amalia's shift is done, racing up the stairs, through hidden passageways through the rock I've discovered.

If she can speak with the Crimson Queen, it changes *everything*.

Which means I need to talk to Os again. I saw the way he looked at her. Like a Dragon seeing a pile of treasure. If I want her help, I need him to agree.

My steps falter as I approach the hallway leading to his door.

The last time I was here...

This is a bad idea. Hesitation gets the best of me, and I turn, only to run right into Amalia. She bounces off me, falling to the floor. I blur, catching her in my arms. Amalia blinks, her blue eyes surprised.

"Thank you, Lord Drayven," her eyes narrow as she pushes away from me.

"Amalia Roth," I smile. "Pleasant, indeed. Be careful where you're going, Amalia Roth. Run into the wrong Fae, and you'll lose your head."

She does not find my jest or my wink amusing.

"Losing my head or speaking to a Drayven?" She wonders aloud. "I think I prefer option one."

Her voice is dripping with sarcasm, making me laugh. Amalia glances around, aware of how loudly we're speaking.

"I've dismissed the guards, don't worry," I say to ease her concerns.

"What privilege you have, Prince," she seethes, thoroughly unimpressed.

"That privilege isn't my status, Amalia," I step forward, and her scent hits me, drawing me in. "It's *power*."

Amalia lets out a shaky breath. "Pretty speech. But from where I stand, you're still a prince. To deny the power of your status would be hypocritical."

Os is the last person who spoke to me like this. It's so refreshing to have someone call me on my bullshit.

Amalia Roth sees right through my mask. Unable to help it, I lean in, hypnotized by her blue eyes and magnetic features.

Then I feel the tip of a dagger at my neck.

"Slow reaction, Prince," she purrs, flashing me a bloodthirsty smile.

Fucking *hell*.

I'm starting to understand why Os is so protective over her.

I match her smile with one of my own, "You've got quite the bite, horse girl. Threatening to kill the Crown Prince *is* treason, you know."

Amalia has every reason to kill me. A very real part of me would accept it if this was it. I'm happy to meet my death at the end of her blade. "Go on, do it. Stab me. Kill the heir to the High Council seat. I think you'll be surprised at what happens next."

Amalia blinks, surprised at my sudden fervor.

She forgets how long I've hung under Achan Drayven's noose. Her anger is merely a drop in the ocean of mine.

I lean in, allowing the blade to break through my skin. It's a risk; a huge one. I know what it will show her.

But something about this, about *her*, it feels different.

"Touch me again," she snarls. "and it'll be the last thing you ever do."

I see the same anger within her that I know lives within me.

"So different from the woman I met in the Annag," I whisper.

"That was before I knew the truth," her face goes cold, and she steps back. "You're just another Drayven bastard."

My laugh is hollow as her words ring true.

"I will give you a piece of advice, Amalia Roth. Never assume that a familial bond equals loyalty."

"Am I supposed to believe you're not loyal to the High Council?"

"Believe whatever you want, Amalia Roth. I have a feeling nobody tells you what to do or what to feel. But look past the obvious. Perhaps you'll find something unexpected."

Before she can stop me, I blur and grab her dagger, using it to slice off a thin section of her silky gray hair. I drop her dagger into her hands and step back, pocketing the strands.

She launches at me with a snarl, but I'm faster and easily avoid her attack.

"Goodbye, Amalia Roth. I'll see you again soon, I'm sure," I turn to walk away but bend down and brush my lips against the edge of her ear and whisper. "A gilded cage is still a cage—it just looks nicer."

"Do that again and see what happens, Prince." She calls after me, but I say nothing in return.

I can feel her presence following me. Before I can think better of it and let my nerves get the best of me again, I walk up to Os' door and knock.

Here goes nothing.

CHAPTER 24
OS

"What do you want, Nyall?"

The Prince smirks.

"Can I come in? We need to talk."

I used to be able to read him, but his walls are so thick, I can't sense his emotions.

I nod and allow him into my room, closing the doors behind him. I don't know how he knows, but that fucking cunt knows that Amalia is an Arkaydian. I can tell. Why else would he be here?

"It's been a long time," Nyall looks around my room. It's the same as it was the last time he was here. This is not my home; there is no reason to get comfortable here.

"Not long enough."

Nyall laughs. "I think you'll disagree when you hear what I have to say."

"I've told you before, I don't give a fuck what you have to say."

"Even if it's about killing my father?"

That stops me in my tracks.

Nyall gives me a knocking smirk. "I thought so. Let's take a seat. This will not be a short conversation."

I take a seat by the fire directly across from Nyall. The Prince snaps his fingers, and I watch as two glasses of amber liquid appear.

"Mead?"

I shake my head. There's no point. Alcohol does not affect Dragons. Our metabolisms are too fast.

Nyall shrugs and brings the glass to his mouth. Setting the glass down on the side table, he leans back and watches me.

He thinks he's in control here. How *adorable*.

"Get on with it," I say, my tone gruff.

Nyall nods, "Over the past two centuries, there has been a growing opposition that wants to depose my Father. A rebellion, if you will."

I grunt. I remember the first rebellion and it didn't end well.

"I have the spells necessary to drain my father of magyk, but in order to kill him, I'll need a distraction."

I lift a brow, still unsure what this has to do with me.

"I need *her*."

I'm out of my seat, my hand around his throat in an instant. Nyall smirks as I squeeze, cutting off his airway.

"You don't get to have her, *boy*," I lean down and hiss in his face but Nyall merely laughs.

Nyall smirks and wheezes, "Tha-that's up to her. Not you."

"You. Can't. Have. Her." I hiss, spitting in his face. "Never. You're not betraying her like you betrayed me."

Nyall blinks in surprise.

Fuck. I said too much. With a snarl, I pull my arm away, allowing him to breathe. I get up off the floor, needing space.

"Stay away from her, Nyall," I warn, but Nyall isn't swayed.

"No," the Prince's smile falls. "I'm afraid I cannot do that...because I need her help."

The cocky Prince is gone. *This* is the young Fae I remember. Sincere...and desperate.

"She will never help you."

"That's her choice though, isn't it?" The Prince's words are pointed.

He's also right.

"Why do you need her help? She's just a human."

Now it's Nyall's turn to laugh.

"You can't *possibly* think I believe that. I just watched her speak to a Dragon. Not just any Dragon either, but the goddamn Crimson Queen."

I'm glad I looked away before Nyall began to speak, so that he can't the surprise on my face.

"How do you know this?" I breathe.

The Prince remains casual and uncaring. "I followed her. I wanted to make sure Achan didn't plan some trap for her in the Pit."

"And why would he do that? She's just a Candidate."

I turn, facing the Prince fully. The firelight plays off his pale skin.

When I first met him, he looked so innocent to the world. But life has hardened him, as it does for us all.

"I would like to speak with her."

"And yet, you came to me."

The Prince nods. "Yes. I've seen the way you act with her. Your Dragon likes her, doesn't it?"

I bare my teeth at him, furious that he can see my emotions that clearly.

Nyall steps closer. "I'm betting there's a bond, there. Let me guess; she's your familiar?"

How the *fuck* does he know that?

"As I thought," the Prince smirks at the surprise on my face. "Your scents are similar. There's a certain spice you each share."

I've kept tabs on Nyall throughout the years. Loosely, but none of them reported back just how talented he's grown. To be able to sense details so minute in someone's magyk is a skill that takes centuries to hone.

"What is this, Nyall? A game you've decided to play because you're bored?"

"On the contrary," he croons. "I've never been more serious. I came to you because you know Amalia, and if you accompany her maybe..." he pauses, suddenly looking nervous. "Maybe Amalia will be more comfortable. She doesn't trust me."

"For good fucking reason, too," I snarl.

Nyall sighs sadly. "She isn't the only one playing their part."

I pause, processing his words.

"Amalia Roth is an Arkaydian pretending to be a human." My heart stops at his words. "Just like I pretend to be loyal to my Father."

Pretty words. But are they true?

"I don't believe you."

Nyall gives me a sad, half smile. "I know you don't, but I'm asking you to try regardless."

"Why?"

Nyall's mismatched eyes are clear and telling. "Because I'm offering you the thing you want most in this world. What *both* of you want most."

"And what that?" I cross my arms.

Nyall takes a deep breath. "Revenge...and your freedom."

Suspicion clouds my mind, but the seriousness in Nyall's words pierces through the darkness.

Freedom.

Is it even possible? I've long given up hoping, but I can feel the sincerity in Nyall's words.

"You're the reason I lost my freedom. I see no reason to trust you with it now."

"Some things never change," Nyall laughs humorlessly. "Whether or not you want to believe me, this is the truth: my father is killing our world, and if we don't stop it, there will be nothing left to save. Don't be a selfish cunt. Ask Amalia. At the very least ask. It's worth the effort."

Something about the *weight* in his words triggers a realization.

"You're their leader, aren't you?" The realization is a heavy weight on my shoulders. "The rebellion."

Nyall nods. "Yes. I have been working on this for two hundred years. This will work, I know it will."

"And you're okay with it? Killing your father?"

Nyall looks at me, his eyes full of pain. With a nod, he stands and begins unbuttoning his shirt.

"What the fuck are you—" the words dry up on my tongue as I take in his bare upper-half.

Oh *Gods.*

CHAPTER 25
NYALL

Os stares at the scars.

Layers and layers of tattoos cover them, but Dragons have incredible eyesight.

I know he can see the bumpy scar tissue down inner arms and on my pecs.

"My legs are the same."

"Did he do that to you?" Os asks in a low voice.

"Some of it. Some...I did to myself."

"Nyall..." Os breathes.

I hold up a hand. "Don't. I'm not here for your pity. I am here because I finally see the truth. Everything you said about him was true."

Os takes a deep breath and runs a hand through his dark, wavy hair.

"What's your plan?"

I knew he'd want details, so I came prepared. Tossing on my shirt, we take a seat and I run through the plan from start to finish, down to disqualifying Dyana and forcing Mirielle and Amalia into the finals.

"I don't know," Os sighs. "The Dragons might not help. They might not talk to her."

I nod. "I know. But we have to try. Can you imagine? If she could win their favor? Win their *help?*"

"What of their fate? Will you leave them here to die?"

Anger runs through me. "You really do think the worst of me, don't you? When my Father is dead, I'll let them go. Every last one of them."

Suspicion and doubt are plain on his face.

With a sigh, I stand. "At least ask her, Os. If she says no, if you *both* say no...I will not ask again. But this is happening with or without you, know that."

Os say nothing, he simply stares at me.

I let out a sigh and walk towards the door.

"I'll ask," his voice surprises me. I pause and glance over my shoulder. "But I make no guarantees, and her choice is my choice."

A tiny kernel of hope is kindled within me.

"Thank you," I bow my head, letting him see the truth within my eyes as our gazes meet. "I will respect whatever choice is made. But *thank you*, Os. Truly."

CHAPTER 26
TARAN

I dislike this place. *Immensely.*

The air smells bad and I've been on edge ever since we arrived.

But the only good part about being in Castael Laryn, outside of watching over my friend Amalia, is Aanad.

Aanad.

I imagine her gorgeous black fur glimmering in the light of the suns. She's perfect, and I must tell her how I feel.

But getting out of this stall will be tricky.

I wait until the suns go down and darkness coats the world before stretching my neck out beyond the door and using my lips to wiggle the latch of my stall.

It drops with a loud clunk and I freeze, my ears twisting to catch any sign that the Fae heard me.

No one notices.

There is another stable here, one for the royal beasts. Aanad told me so when we met. I'm not sure Amalia knows it exists, but it's here.

I carefully ease my stall door open and walk into the aisle, leaving the common stable and heading towards the castle. My hooves plop quietly in the dirt. I'm a big horse, so "quiet" isn't something that comes easily to me. But for Aanad, I try.

It takes awhile to walk around the castle. I get distracted by some rather tantalizing looking shrubs that taste delicious. Munching away, I get to the south side of the Black Citadel.

It's hideous. Not that anyone cares about a horse's opinion.

The royal stables are empty, most of the stalls unoccupied. But a quiet whinny makes its way to me and my ears turn forward.

Aanad!

She peeks her beautiful head out of her stall at the far end and neighs when she sees me.

"What are you doing here?" she asks. *"You'll get caught!"*

Animals can communicate with each other through more than sounds. I can read her meaning from her body language and the way her ears twist and turn. Even from the flaring of her nostrils.

"I...wanted to see you," I neigh back, making sure not to be too loud.

Aanad snorts. *"Well hurry up, then. We should get out of here before we get caught. The mortals would be very upset if they found out we have the ability to escape."*

Excitement races through me as I walk towards her stall. Using the same method that opened my own stall door, I lean forward and unlock the latch to her stall with my lips.

It silently opens and Aanad walks out.

I'm in awe of her.

Her body is all muscle. She exudes strength and confidence.

"Follow me," she nickers. But as she passes me, she rubs her face against my neck, sniffing me.

Oh my goodness. My entire body tingles as she continues on. I watch her with wide eyes, enamored. Without even thinking about it, I follow her.

I've never had a mate.

I've known many horses who found theirs. But...no mare has ever taken interest in me. Nor any geldings.

Not that I care one way or the other. Love is love, even for an animal.

But I've never found love outside of the love of my herd.

Amalia.

Dyana.

My family. My *herd*.

Aanad walks for a bit, and I eye her gorgeous backside and the sway of her luscious black tail.

She stops after walking through a small opening in the wall surrounding the city.

"I do not want to go too far," she nickers. *"Should my person need me."*

I nod my head and approach her until we're staring at each other face to face.

She nuzzles her cheek against mine and I nearly fall over.

Aanad is careful to avoid poking me with the sharp ruby horn on her forehead that flickers in and out of existence.

"Why did you come?" she asks, leaning in closer. I tentatively reach forward until my lips hover above her soft mane. Leaning in, I take my teeth and begin grooming her. Itching the spots for her that she is unable to reach herself.

Aanad sighs in pleasure.

I love that sound.

"Do you not know?" I snort quietly. *"You are beautiful."*

She lets out a deep breath and I almost jump when her teeth meet my mane. Aanad begins grooming me back.

The truest sign of affection amongst our kind.

"Do you like me, Taran?"

My eyes almost bulge out of my head. I'm scared to answer, but the feeling of her grooming me is so delightful, I can't help but be honest.

"I do," I breathe. *"But...do you have a mate? I do not want to cause problems."*

Aanad stops grooming me for a moment and steps back. I do the same, mirroring her actions.

She twines her neck with mine, in our version of a hug.

"No," she nickers quietly. *"The others are...scared of me. They think I'm too strong. That I might hurt them or any young we have."*

I rear my head back and narrow my eyes, flaring my nostrils in anger.

"How dare they! There is nothing wrong with a strong mare. You are perfect just the way you are. It is them who are wrong, Aanad. I will bite anyone who says otherwise. In the butt."

She laughs at my anger and nuzzles closer.

"No one has ever defended me before," she pauses. *"It is very nice of you, Taran."*

Nice. Nice. Is that good?

"I like you too," she nickers, and I do stumble a bit.

Forcing my legs to balance, I take a deep breath. But my blood is racing and my heart is pounding.

I have to ask. Stepping back, I angle my head so that we're eye to eye.

"Would you be my mate, my beautiful Aanad? With your gorgeous fur and your beautiful ruby eyes. I will always protect you and share my carrots with you, for as long as we live."

Aanad's tongue hits my cheek as she licks me.

"Yes, I think I would like that, Taran."

Ohmygodsohmygods. SHE SAID YES!

I want to let out the loudest neigh in the world, but hold back for fear that it alerts the guards.

A question comes to mind. Something I've always wanted but...never have had anyone to ask.

"Mate?" I nicker, and Aanad licks me again happily.

"Yes?"

"Do you, um, do you know how to speak to them?"

Aanad leans back and flares her nostrils. *"What do you mean?"*

"The two-legs. Do you know how to speak to them?"

I'm sure she doesn't.

Most animals don't. But Aanad seems so smart, and Oryx are known across the animal kingdom for being incredibly smart and magical.

I have to try.

Aanad snorts. *"I do. But I do not speak to them, even though I can."*

I don't ask why she doesn't, for its none of my business and likely something she does to protect herself.

Keeping Aanad safe, keeping my family safe; that's all that matters.

"Could you teach me? Their words are...difficult to say."

Aanad nods. *"They are. It's part of why I do not speak to them. I find their language difficult. But I know enough to teach you."*

Gratitude bursts from me and I lick her cheek.

"Thank you, my beautiful mate."

"Who do you wish to speak to?" she asks as we adjust and get back to grooming each other.

The moons shine brightly above our heads.

I could stay here forever.

"I would like to speak to my person. Amalia."

"The gray-haired woman who rides you?"

I grunt in affirmation.

"She is an Arkaydian, is she not?" Aanad asks.

"She is. She will hear my thoughts. But I need to know the language to think them in."

"I see," Aanad replies. *"Then I will teach you, and you will speak with her. I like this Amalia. Her magyk feels nice."*

I move my head up and down in agreement.

Amalia's magyk is like a warm hug. It instantly makes me feel safe.

We spend the rest of the night talking. Aanad teaches me how to say words in the language of the two-legs, so that someday soon, I can tell Amalia that she is my herd. My *family*.

"You have a big heart," Aanad says. *"I am glad I met you, Taran. Very, very glad."*

"I'm glad I met you too, my beautiful Aanad."

Life is short and this world has grown dangerous. I want my person to know how I feel.

I want Amalia to know that I love her *too*.

Images of Amalia's bloody, battered face run through my head on repeat.

When I entered the mess hall to find Amalia and Reymand in a fight, I almost blacked out.

My rage was so great, I could barely breathe. My chest is still tight as the adrenaline racing through my body fuels the fury.

He put his *hands* on Amalia. He hurt my familiar.

KILL HIM. FEAST ON HIS FLESH AND CARVE OUT HIS BONES. I agree with my Beast. That sounds like an excellent idea. Amalia follows closely behind. Her spiced pomegranate scent in the air makes my already fraying patience snap.

I blur, grabbing one of the chairs in the sitting area and fling it into the wall. The wood shatters, sending splinters and broken chunks throughout the room.

"He *hurt* you," I snarl, ready to destroy the remainder of my furniture.

"Reymand?" Amalia asks, walking over to me. She should be afraid, but there isn't an ounce of fear in her pale blue eyes. "Os, I egged him on. He said something rude to Dyana and I snapped. I *wanted* him to hurt me, that way I had a legitimate reason to beat the shit out of him."

DON'T CARE. HE HURT HER. HE HURT WHAT IS OURS!

"He hurt you," I hiss. "Your jaw is barely healed. It hurts, doesn't it? I bet you can barely talk, you idiot. What were you thinking, pushing him into a fight?"

"He did, but I was fine. Clearly, since I bested him in one move. I'm not your property, Os, you don't have the right to say who can touch me and who can't."

There's a second when the world turns sharp as my Beast takes over. I tilt my head back to the ceiling and let out a loud roar, making the walls shake.

When the Beast is done, a quiet descends. Amalia stands before me, watching with arms crossed; still not afraid.

"I'm not saying you're my fucking property, Amalia." I don't mean to sound harsh, but every day it's getting harder and harder to hold back.

I have to tell her the truth.

Amalia glares at me, "I don't need anyone to defend me."

"Bullshit. You DO need someone to defend you because you're still holding back!" The Beast bursts back into my head and I let out another roar.

She thinks I don't know.

But I am old. Old enough, I remember when the Gods walked openly in our world. Old enough to know that Amalia Roth's magyk smells like the Morrigyn's.

Her blood tastes like divinity.

Amalia is God touched.

A God touched Arkaydian. And something else I do not recognize.

"I'm not holding back, Os. I'm being careful; there's a difference," she whispers in my mind as I pace at the far end of the room, trying to get my anger under control.

"Bullshit," I turn, meeting her pale gaze. *"That is total bullshit Amalia."*

"Bullshit?" Amalia's face turns furious and I prepare for the onslaught of cruelty she's about to sling my way.

"You wanna know what's bullshit? The fact that you're friends with Crown Prince Nyall Drayven. You lied to us. You said you're not any friend to the Fae, so imagine my surprise to see you greeting him like an old friend last night."

Ah. The fight drains from me.

I nearly tore Nyall's head off at the way he was drenched in her scent. No wonder it was so strong. She was still there.

I'm struck silent, debating how much to confess about my relationship with the Prince.

"I came back to your room after stable duty yesterday. We ran into each other and when he left, I decided to follow him because I don't trust a word he says. I watched him saunter his pompous ass right into your room, Os. What the hell?"

I snarl and pace towards the fire.

"I don't trust a word he says either; make no mistake, Amalia."

The tone in my voice makes her pause. "You and the Prince aren't friends then?"

"I would rather stick my head in a wasp nest than be friends with that prick."

"Why was he in here, then?" she asks, her tone kinder and full of curiosity.

This truth is one I wish I didn't have the obligation to share. I'd much rather keep Amalia as far away from the Fae as possible, *him* included.

"Nyall wasn't here to talk to me...he was here because he wants to talk to you."

Amalia blinks, "I'm sorry; what did you just say?"

"The Prince would like to meet with *you*."

"He came here to talk to you, to ask for a meeting with me?"

I sigh. *I fucking wish he hadn't.*

"Yes."

"But...why did he come to you and not just find me himself?"

"Nyall...would like your help. Our help, actually. He wants to talk to me, too."

Cold laughter bursts out of Amalia's mouth. "What world is the Prince living in that he thinks I would ever help him? I would rather die than help a Drayven.

I sniff. "I agree."

"What did you say to him?" I turn, facing her fully as Amalia takes a seat in one of the undestroyed chairs by the fire.

"I told him he's a spoiled little prick, and I wish I had torn out his throat when I had the chance."

"So you do know each other."

Our eyes meet. "Unfortunately. Speaking of, how do you know him, little spark?"

Annoyance enters her gaze. Amalia leans back and lets out a deep sigh. "If you must know, it was when I went out for a ride. I didn't know who he was at the time."

Hmm.

"Not friends then, I take it?" She smirks.

"*Decidedly* not. I would rather rip out my claws."

Amalia winces a bit at the grotesque imagery. "Why do you hate him so much?"

Because I didn't hate him at all...until he betrayed me. Until he stood there as his father ate my hatchlings in front of me. Until he broke my heart and the last remaining bit of trust left in me.

Instead, I look at the far wall, "I don't want to talk about it."

"Okay," Amalia accepts my response. "So you told him no then."

"I told him I would speak to you first and support whatever you decided."
I turn my head back towards her until our eyes meet.

Surprise is all over Amalia's face.

She really doesn't know, does she?

"Why?" Amalia asks, clearly not understanding.

"Because the whole thing was," I pause, searching for the right word, "odd.
I think Nyall was serious. He seemed worried and frantic. And he knows
how I feel about his father. I've never been quiet about my dislike. If he
came here, it means his father doesn't know about it. Whatever this is, it's
not the High Council. And that makes me curious."

"Curious?"

"Something felt different. I'm not sure what."

"Well obviously my answer is no," Amalia declares.

I nod. "I'll let him know."

Amalia cocks her head, inspecting me without shame.

"You hate him...why?"

I cannot lie to her. I land on an answer that is truthful, without giving too
much away.

"I could smell you on him. I almost killed him on the spot. That's why I
pulled him into the room. I wanted to ensure no one would witness as I
flayed his skin from his flesh."

Amalia blinks. "That's extreme. You were that mad because he smelled like
me?"

SEE ME. SEE THE TRUTH.

"Look, I'm trying here," she says with frustration. "I'm trying to trust you. I believe you about Nyall; I can see how much you dislike him. It's hard, but...I'm trying. Okay? Now, I think if you shared, it might help. So why did that make you so mad, Os? Why do you want to flay someone for smelling like me?"

I carefully enter her mind and she lets me.

"You know I'm a shifter," I say carefully. Amalia nods and I crouch down in front of her, going down on my knees. I lift a hand a trace lines across her legs, needing to be grounded by the heat coming off her skin.

This is still new, so I'm unsure it will work, but I allow my humanity to fade and my Beast come to the surface.

I force my eyes to shift, revealing to her the truth of my nature.

"I will always be mad when someone hurts you, A gahrá, because according to my Beast, we're familiars."

Amalia's heart stops for a moment, before bursting into a frantic staccato.

Shit. She's panicking. I pull the Beast back and it goes willingly, ashamed and embarrassed. Amalia jumps to her feet and runs out of the room.

"I can feel your panic, A gahrá. Please just list—" I try, but she shoves me out of her head. It feels like a slap to my brain.

"Tell the Prince I'll meet with him. But I promise nothing," she says without looking. For someone with relatively short legs, she walks fast, almost jogging out of the Dragon Pit. I keep up with her, refusing to let her go through this alone.

"Amalia, please."

I can hear her blood rushing faster as her blood pressure skyrockets. Her scent grows stronger, even as we emerge into the fresh air of the courtyard.

Amalia breaks out into a jog, heading straight for the stables. Her large white draft horse, Taran, whinnies a hello before his ears flick and his eyes go wide.

He's feeling her panic.

She leaps onto his back, no tack or bridle.

"Fast, Taran. Get me outside of the city. I need to be alone," Amalia whispers to her horse in a frantic voice. He neighs softly and breaks into a trot.

"Amalia, please. It's not safe for you to go out alone," I try to get through her mental walls but it's no use.

She's gone.

Pain encompasses my entire being and I watch as my familiar, as the other half of my soul, *rejects* me.

CHAPTER 28
TARAN

My friend is sad.

I gallop towards the Annag, feeling Amalia's pain.

Amalia is my friend. I do not want her to be afraid.

Her fear increases my own. I'm always on edge already, especially in this area of the Kingdom. But feeling Amalia's panic makes my own heart race alongside hers.

We reach the forest and I slow into a canter, weaving through the branches and leaping over logs.

It reminds me of home.

I *miss* home. But Amalia needs me.

My friend needs me.

Slowing into an easy trot, we continue through the forest for almost half an hour until we reach a small creek.

Amalia slides off my back, stumbling over to the water. I follow, meandering behind and lowering my head to the water for a drink. The cold, refreshing water hits my tongue and I gulp it down happily.

I miss life in the forest. I miss Twyn Fells. But I would miss my friend Amalia more.

Amalia takes care of me and my friends. She takes care of everyone around her, but has no one to take care of her.

I will take care of my friend.

Amalia kneels in the water, grounding herself with the cold. My own head feels clearer.

Eventually, I notice her small, furless body begin to shiver.

Two-legs are so delicate. My hooves splash as I plop into the water slowly, making sure not to trip on the slick rocks of the riverbed.

With my teeth, I grab the back of her shirt and back up, dragging her out of the water. I let go when we reach the dry ground.

A strange noise comes out of her. A panicked, sad sound. Amalia's eyes begin to leak. She collapses to the ground with a pained wail.

"It's not supposed to be like this. It wasn't supposed to be like this. WHY DID YOU DO THIS TO ME?"

My friend is upset. Something happened. Perhaps she finally noticed the thread.

It's always been there.

A thread of gold, right in the middle of her chest, trailing off. I never knew what it was trailing off to until I met the Oryx.

Beautiful Aanad.

That gold string tied to her rider. Nyall something? I do not remember. Maybe this is what my friend is sad about.

"They were supposed to be here for this, Taran."

Amalia looks up at me, her face damp and her eyes glossy.

"They were supposed to help me find my familiar. How am I supposed to do this without them? How am I supposed to do any of this when they're dead?"

"I'm here," I try to say, but it comes out as a nicker. She cannot understand my language fully, but she understands what I mean.

I lay down carefully as to not bump into her. Craning my neck around her body, I push my snout against her cheek. She wraps her arms around my head, leaning her weight into me.

Her cheeks smell salty.

Oh, salt! I love salt.

My tongue darts out as I lick my friend's cheek. This leaking water tastes delicious.

Eventually, her cheek dries and the salt disappears, so I stop. My friend Amalia leans into me as her heartbeat slows and the panic ebbs.

I feel my own panic fade away as my heart slows too. Amalia does not know it, but she and her dark-haired friend are my herd.

I have never had a herd of my own before.

"I miss them so much sometimes it feels like I can't even breathe. I know I have Dyana, but...sometimes I still feel so alone. How am I supposed to go on when they're gone, Taran?" Amalia whispers into my fur.

I push my snout against her cheek and focus as hard as I can. I do not have much magyk, but all horses have a spark.

A spark is all it takes.

I send my friend a wave of magyk, the way she does to me.

Amalia's arms fall and she pulls back, looking at me with wide eyes.

I've got you, friend. With a groan, I straighten my legs and stand. I pull my left leg beneath me and bow, making it easier for my friend to slide onto my back.

With a deep breath, I try something.

"Fam—lee. Tahr-an fam—lee." The letters feel strange inside my head. But I try to mimic how she sounds. I send it through our bond, hoping it works.

I feel her shock. "Taran, how...?"

"Lo-love," I force the words out, even though it's difficult. *"I talk be-caus I love."*

That pained, sad noise bursts from her chest again. My friend Amalia leans down and wraps her arms around my neck. I crane my head back and rub my cheek against hers.

"Yes, Taran, you are my family. I am yours, and you are mine. I will always love you."

I did it. She understood me! My herd. My family. I try to say this but my energy is spent, so it's a low nicker instead.

"You make me feel less alone," Amalia whispers.

"Ama not allonee. Never allonee." Even though I'm exhausted, I force the words to form in my head. My friend feels alone! I must show her that she is not.

"You're right, I'm not alone. I just...I never expected this. Never dared hope. Ever since they died, it's just been about staying alive. It still is. But now...it's all gotten so complicated, Taran. There's so much on the line, and I'm so afraid. If I fail, if I can't do this, then everyone dies. I can't...I can't lose anyone else, Taran. Sometimes, I'm so scared that I can't even breathe."

I concentrate hard. *"Ama bray-v. Ama strong. Ama kind."*

She laughs lightly, *"I'm trying, Taran. I'm trying to be brave. But it's so hard. I'm so tired."*

We fall silent on the walk back to the city. In no hurry, I plod slowly, pausing every so often to munch on some rather tasty looking winter grass. It's a bit dry, but the flavor is warm and sweet.

We emerge into the open and I gather my courage.

My herd needs me to be strong.

I will not fail my family now.

CHAPTER 29
OS

"Again," I demand.

Amalia is exhausted, but that's just because she's not used to wielding her magyk.

She's hidden it, and in turn, it's weakened, as has her control over it. The first few weeks of training like this, physical or Magykal, are always the hardest.

"One more time and then we're done. But now use your magyk and when you push in, push OUT towards me with it."

"Okay," she huffs.

I close my eyes and watch as she gathers her magyk—a golden arrow suddenly hits me straight in my chest. It moved so fast, I couldn't track it in my mind's eye. My eyes flare open as I'm thrown into the air.

I flip and twist midair, hitting the wall with my hip but landing on my feet.

Amalia's eyes open at the sound and she blinks at the sight of me so far away.

"Very good. It seems you have some bite after all." She blushes at my words. "Less power next time, but good."

There's a knock on the door and Amalia jumps at the sound.

"Peace, A gahrá. It's just the servants bringing food."

She looks down, her cheeks flushed, but this time from embarrassment.

I retrieve the food and set it down in front of us. It's a massive tray of fresh fruits, meats, and cheeses.

"Eat. You need it. Magyk burns twice the energy as regular exercise. The more you use it, the more fuel you need to put in your body."

We're quiet for a few minutes as we both dig in. I didn't realize how hungry I was either.

"When did you know?" Her words shock me so much I nearly let the piece of cured ham fall out of my mouth.

"The...familiar thing," she clarifies. "When did you realize?"

I can feel her fear and nervousness in asking this. She's scared I'm going to be angry at the rejection.

Seeing her leave...it hurt.

It still does. But I will not force this.

At least I no longer have to pretend. She knows the truth. She also knows what I am.

I sigh, "My Beast knew the moment I got your scent. But I...didn't want to believe it. It wasn't until the day outside the stables that I knew for sure."

No more hiding.

"You mean when you healed me.."

"Yes," I say, my throat suddenly tight. Am I...nervous too? "I don't actually have healing magyk, Amalia."

She blinks, clearly confused. "My kind can only heal our own kin," I continue. "It's not considered a power; it is simply part of our nature. The only exception is if we manage to form a familiar bond. Then, and only then, can we heal someone outside of our own species. I saw you hurt and my magyk reacted, well, quite strongly. That's when I realized it wanted to heal you. My Beast, it demanded that I heal you even if it drained me of every drop of power I possess."

If she wasn't my familiar, I wouldn't have been able to heal her. But I...suspected some sort of bond, even before that.

"You—" I stumble over my words, wanting desperately to get this right and not push her further away. "You don't have to accept the familiar bond, Amalia."

She's quiet.

"I will never force you to accept it. I can't, actually. An Arkaydian is the only one who can complete the bond, so you don't need to worry, please."

She nods a little and chews on her bottom lip. "What happens if I reject it?"

The color drains from my face, and I close my eyes as I struggle to compose myself. After taking a deep breath, I open my eyes slowly and look at her.

"Nothing. You can reject it if that's what you want. But it means I'll never find another familiar. Arkaydians can form unlimited familiar bonds."

Amalia goes still. "Interesting."

I shift my glance away for a moment. "Yes. But for me, there will only ever be one chance."

"So, this is your only chance to bond...*ever?*"

I nod, "Yes. For us...there is only one."

Amalia gulps nervously, "How long do I have until I need to... um, decide?"

"There is no time limit, A gahrá. I've lived for centuries. I've seen kingdoms rise and fall. I've seen peace and I've been to war. None of that comes even close to how I feel about you. You're in my soul, Amalia. I would wait a lifetime and then some if that's what you need."

Amalia blinks away her tears, "And what happens if I accept? My...my parents told me some of it, but it was so long ago that it's a little blurry."

The corner of my mouth raises in a half smile, "If you accept, we would be bound together for the rest of our lives. You would gain my lifespan, as well as some of my power. I could heal you from great distances, and you, me—and when you die, I will die with you."

Her eyes widen at this knowledge, and I feel her dismay.

"I am not afraid of death, A gahrá," I say softly. "But you are safe. If I die, you will continue on. There is a reason Arkaydians were revered. Their magyk is unlike anything else in the world. You would, however, feel my death."

"Feel it?"

I hesitate before nodding, "Yes."

Amalia sighs, leaning back in her chair as she inspects the ceiling.

"What else?"

"Both of our magyks would get a boost. Our...life forces would merge into one, and with that, we would both have access to each other's magyk, should the other will it."

"You could use my power, you mean?"

I nod.

"If I make it out of here alive," she hesitates, "then I will think about it."

"You're not going to die." I grab her hands with a snarl. "I won't allow it."

"You don't know that," Amalia looks down, meeting my gaze with a sad sort of clarity. "Nor can you make me that promise. Even if you wish it to be false, we both know there's a high chance that I will die in the Arena, Os. That's the reality of the Gauntlet, and no power or magyk can change it now."

I close my eyes as the sadness hits.

She's right.

"You're right, but I'm going to do everything in my power to ensure that you win."

We stay like that, hand in hand, for a few minutes. The feel of the cold stone mixed with the heat of her body and the blazing fire is soothing.

Eventually, Amalia sighs. I let go of her hand and we stand, staring into each other's eyes.

I cup lift a hand and cup Amalia's cheek. Her skin is cold and soft beneath my palm. "You don't need to say it. I know."

I let go of her face and drop my hand to place it over her heart.

Amalia gasps at the touch. "Yesterday...it wasn't about you. Someday I'll be ready to talk about it, but not now. I just...I need you to know it wasn't about you, and I'm sorry for running."

It doesn't erase the hurt, but it dulls the blow. "I know, A gahrá. I am in your soul. Just...know that you never have to run from me."

"You would really wait for me?" The words are barely a whisper.

I look into her beautiful blue eyes and nod. "Can't you see? I would wait an eternity for you, little spark."

"If only we had that much time." Her voice cracks and stray tear drops down her cheek. I brush it away.

"We will, I swear it."

"Thank you, for—"

"I understand, Amalia. I see you and accept you for all that you are. You don't need to explain yourself to me. You never need to explain."

I learn down until we're forehead to forehead.

"I see you, A gahrá," Her pomegranate scent invades my senses. She's everywhere, all around me and inside my bones.

I press a soft kiss to her forehead, *"I see you for all that you are and all that you aren't. I see your heart and all of your broken pieces. I accept you just as you are."*

I feel her heart begin to race as the panic nears. Too much emotion and Amalia Roth crumbles.

She steps back, pulling out of my embrace as her eyes turn chilly.

"Nyall wants to meet after the Fray tomorrow." I blurt out, wanting her to stay longer.

Her jaw clenches, "I'm bringing Dyana and Mirielle."

"Good," I smirk. "That will throw him off."

Amalia nods, turning and walking towards the door. She grabs the metal handle, glancing back over her shoulder

"Goodnight, Os."

Stay.

Stay, please.

"Goodnight, A gahrá."

CHAPTER 30

OS

Thump. Thump. Thump.

I do not know why my heart continues to beat. I do not know how such a thing is possible as my sword slices through the throat of a scared, tortured Dragon, as I kill my *kin,* I wonder if there is anything left of me worth saving.

The bout ended quickly, and I moved to the stands, craving Amalia like the desert craves water. I stand in the audience of the Fray, covered in blood, dirt, and sweat, I stare into the eyes of my freedom. My savior. My *familiar.*

And my *hope* stares back, with eyes of ice and flame. The moment I noticed Amalia was starting to panic, I began trying desperately to connect with her. But our magyk lessons have worked too well. I know she can *feel* me at the edge of her mind, but she locks me out.

She locks. Me. Out.

The raging Beast inside of me claws at my skin, begging to be let out.

It wants to take Amalia far away and hide her away from the world.

The crowd doesn't notice, nor does the High Council thankfully, but Amalia's panic begins to change.

She glances away from me, turning her attention back to the Dragon before us. I *feel* her magyk roil and rumble, growing bigger and bigger until it disappears.

No, not disappear; it just...*moved.*

The audience watches as the Crimson Queen lets out a massive roar and charges her opponent—a brown dragon named Abaloth.

The Queen was injured, fatally so. But the wounds are *gone*. Still there, but they no longer freely bleed.

Moreover, there is new *life* in the Queen's eyes.

Amalia Roth very well might be the one to save us all. Who else can *connect* with Dragons in this way?

For the first time in a long time, I have hope, and it's because of *her*.

"Have any plans this evening?" Ireyna's voice drips with lust. She's hanging off my arm and every fiber of my being wants to shove her away, but *that* would lead to questions and attention, both of which are things I don't want.

What I want is to shout at Amalia for locking me out, spank her on her perfect, tight little ass, and then fuck her until we both forget our names.

Not being able to do so because we have an appointment with the Crown Fucking Prince is making me a bit cranky.

"We are talking about what happened tonight. Particularly the part when you knew how to lock me out." I shove into Amalia's head and this time she lets me in.

"Looks like you're a little busy right now." She catches my eye before looking pointedly at Ireyna hanging off my arm. *"Do enjoy your evening."*

Amalia pushes me out of her mind so hard, it feels like a slap to my senses.

"I gotta go. See you later," I tell Ireyna, wiggling out from her grasp. I walk faster, catching up to Amalia.

Mirielle and Dyana follow as well.

"We have business to attend to," I snarl.

I'm not actually angry. I'm scared. Terrified, actually. I want to explain it all, but our time here is short.

Annoyed at the world, I shove open the doors to my room, knowing Nyall would already be there.

Sure thing, the Prince is sitting in a chair near my fireplace, sipping from a crystal glass full of honey wine. Those mismatched eyes slowly look our way as a slight smirk plays on a face bathed in warm firelight.

"Drayven," I hiss.

~~Yes. Take it out on him. He understands why you're mad. He gets it.~~

"Breaking and entering, now? Is being an arrogant, rich prick not enough for you?" My words are poisonous barbs, but Nyall doesn't take the bait.

He knows what I'm doing, and that only annoys me further.

Nyall nods, lifting his glass of wine in a toast. "Congratulations on another victory, old friend."

My patience shatters.

I'm before him, slapping the glass out of his hand a moment later. It shoots to the floor before exploding, sending shards of glass scattering about the ground.

The Prince just laughs.

"We are not friends," I remind him, getting in his face. "Get on with this. I'm tired and your presence is unwelcome."

I can't sit. Not right now. Instead, I stand next to the fireplace, leering down at him, while Amalia takes a seat in a chair nearby.

"Why, Os, surely you've told your friends here how many centuries we've known each other?"

Oh, that mother*fucker.*

I'm about to rip him a new asshole when Amalia raises her hand, stopping me.

Without hesitation, I obey her command. My Dragon purrs in satisfaction, happy to follow our familiar's will.

"You're pissing him off on purpose," Amalia raises a brow, seeing right through the Prince's act. "You know what, Os is right. Your presence is unwanted, so how about I make this easy; I don't trust a single word out of your mouth anyways, half-breed. I know you're trying to shock me into trusting you, but it's not going to work so cut the act."

"Ah, the horse girl has some bite, then," Nyall smirks.

I snap my teeth at him, "Get on with it, Drayven."

Nyall sighs and his face goes hard, all emotion gone. It's startling to see. Nyall bows his head, turning to face Amalia. "I need each of you to give a blood oath. What is spoken here must not be repeated."

"You're out of your damn mind if you think we're taking a blood oath with you, Fae. Over my dead, godsdamn body," I shout, furious that this was his plan.

"Then you all will die."

It's the *manner* in which Nyall says this that makes us go quiet.

There's a seriousness in his words that, somehow, we all understand.

"Explain," I demand.

"As much as you can, at least." Mirielle says, surprising me.

She's...defending him. Hmm. I let the thought go for now, but I do not forget it.

Nyall clicks his tongue and begins, "I can say this much. The world is dying. You've all seen it, felt it. This is just the beginning. It will get worse. The forests will die, the Midheym Sea will eventually dry up. Horrible storms will destroy the land before plunging us into a winter so cold, no one will survive. There will be nothing left."

"How do you know this?" Amalia asks, suspicion plain in her voice.

"I can't say anything further because I'm warded from telling anyone who isn't related to me by blood. My father thought he was being smart, but he didn't realize that if someone drinks my blood, the ward considers them family. Hence the need for the blood oath."

"Fine," Amalia snarls, shocking me. "But only if that blood oath protects us, too. You will swear to never tell a soul about our meeting or anything discussed in this room. The blood oath will ensure you uphold that promise, or it will kill you."

Pride warms me. *That's my girl.*

Dyana sputters for a moment but then pauses and takes a deep breath. "Okay. Okay. If he promises too, I'll take the blood oath."

"As will I," Mirielle pipes in, clasping Dyana's hand tightly.

Amalia looks at me, a question in her gaze.

I give her a soft smile. "I follow your decision, *A gahrá.*"

Her cheeks turn pink, and I watch as she hides a shy smile.

Nyall nods, withdrawing a sharp dagger. The hilt is braided black steel inlaid with rubies that shine in the firelight. The blade is rather large for a dagger, but the edge is wicked sharp. Nyall slices it across the meat of his palm and lets it drip into an empty wine glass. Using the unwounded hand, Nyall flicks his finger, and ropes of white magyk seal up the wound with a wet sound. Nyall tosses the dagger at me. I catch it without looking.

"The spell requires three drops of your blood. All of you."

I use the dagger to slash open my palm. The wound gapes and blood spills across my hand. I let it drip into the chalice. It burns and sizzles as it falls, once, twice, three times.

Grabbing the dagger, I walk over to where Amalia sits, going down on one knee in front of her chair. Her pupils dilate at the sight of me on my knees before her.

As I lift the dagger, another idea, a *crazy, impossible* idea runs through my mind.

I drop the dagger and imagine my claws emerging. It hurts for a moment, like it's *almost* too much.

Then I feel the pain of shifting. Shock runs through me as my nails begin to turn black, lengthening into sharp, dangerous claws.

Gently, ever so gently, I drag the claw across Amalia's palm, cradling her hand within my own.

I bring her hand over the glass, letting three drops join the rest, never taking my eyes off her.

For a moment, it's just the two of us.

Try to heal her again! my Beast roars at me.

I concentrate on her wound and send my magyk out.

Even though our familiar bond is unfinished, my magyk jumps into action, excited to mingle with hers. I use it to seal the flesh on her palm and we both look down, watching as the skin knits back together and the blood dries up.

Meeting her gaze, I bring her bloody hand to my mouth and lick.

Sweet pomegranate and rich spices explode on my tongue. Heat rushes through my body at the taste of her blood. It's like being struck by lightning.

"I am with you," I whisper in her head as my lips and tongue finish cleaning her hand.

"I'm still mad at you," she says back. Even in her thoughts, her voice trembles.

"How interesting," Nyall notes, amused. The sound of his voice snaps us back into the moment and I stand, handing the chalice to Dyana and Mirielle before moving to stand behind Amalia, one hand on her shoulder.

I need to touch her. I need to feel her heat.

We watch in tense silence as Mirielle helps Dyana slice her palm before tearing a piece of fabric off her tunic and wrapping it around the cut. Mirielle slices her own hand open after that, letting three drops of blood fall with the rest. She quickly passes the chalice back to us and rips another piece of fabric off, pressing it to her own wound.

"Take a sip and repeat after me." Nyall nods.

I glare at the Prince and shove the chalice into his hand, being careful not to spill anything. "You first, Drayven."

Nyall rolls his eyes but brings the glass to his lips and takes a small sip, **"Blood spilled, blood bound. I vow to not tell another soul what is said upon this hour."**

I blink at how simple the spell is. But, it's to the point. Each of us takes the chalice and repeats the words, one by one.

"Blood spilled, blood bound. I vow to not tell another soul what is said upon this hour."

Mirielle goes last. As she takes a sip of the blood, a sharp snap of magyk echoes through the room and we all jolt as the blood oath settles into place. A glowing silver string connects us all for a brief moment and then it's gone.

"Why are we here, Prince?" Amalia's words echo into the space as Nyall's smile drops. He leans back, crossing one leg over the other as he stretches his right arm over the arm of the chair and rubs his mouth with his left.

"I want you to join the rebellion and help me overthrow the High Council." We all blink as Nyall leans forward, looking me dead in the eyes. "Help me kill my father, Amalia Roth."

CHAPTER 31

NYALL

I knew she would say no.

Still. I didn't realize how much it would hurt to have her laugh in my face about it.

The Gauntlet has officially begun and it's a fucking bloodbath.

Amalia is doing well. Too well. My father is beginning to get suspicious. There's only so much I can do to redirect his attention. Only so many comments about her being a boring, nobody little human until he gets curious.

It's the day before the semi-finals and something feels...off. I've been on edge all day. There's a tightness in my chest. Like my heart is being squeezed within a giant fist. I can't sit still, so I decide to take a walk through the city. Anything to get out of the fucking Citadel.

As I wander through the streets, ignoring the stares and whispers, my thoughts drift to Amalia...and to her familiar. Every time I close my eyes, I see them. I see their hate. Normally the hatred of others only makes me want to try less. Do less.

But them...they are different. They make me want to be better. To try harder and *deserve* my title. It's been a long time since I wanted to make anyone proud.

As I approach the stables, the hot, metallic tang of iron hits me.

I see the blood next. It's everywhere.

The stables are empty and—

Oh *fuck*. Please don't be true. The stables are empty…which usually means the soldiers got hungry.

A strangled sound leaves me as I turn the corner for the last stall and find the mangled, bloody body of Amalia's horse.

Dead Fae lay on the ground next to it.

Footsteps sound behind me.

"Prince Drayven, I'm sorry you had to see this—"

I'm facing the guard, my hand around his neck a moment later. I squeeze tightly, tight enough to cut his airway off.

"Where. Is. She?" I ask with deadly calm. Everything turns sharp and the background fades.

The Fae trembles in my hands.

"D-dungeons," the Fae gasps, choking on his own spit.

"Have you told my father yet?"

"N-no. S-soon."

"Who is supposed to deliver the news to him?"

"Me," the Fae shakes so hard, I can feel his bones vibrating.

"Ah, good then."

I squeeze my fist tighter and tear out his throat in a single move. The guard's spine shatters beneath my grip and blood sprays, drenching my face.

I make the elven symbol for *"clean"* on my palm and the blood goes away. I quickly draw up a spell to get rid of the body and the rest of the blood. No one will notice a bloody body floating down the river.

No one that matters, at least.

But Amalia's horse...Taran, was his name I believe.

I draw up a more complex spell, one that strains on my low reserves. Pushing through the pain, I craft a spell to dislodge a large pile of dirt; he needs to be buried.

I pick a spot near the Annag, just by the river, where I first met Amalia.

Weaving the rest of the spell, I transport his body into the hole and cover it with the loose dirt.

I will bring Amalia here and we will give him a proper send off. But for now, his body is safe and away from the prying hands of the Fae.

Dropping the spell, I shake off the exhaustion it brings and quickly make my way to the Citadel.

She'll still be in the dungeons, I'm sure.

I walk fast, but not so fast as to draw attention. I've gotten very good over the centuries at riding that fine line.

It takes a few minutes to make it down to the dungeons. The Citadel is as deep as it is tall. The underground levels spiral down deep into the ground. Prisoners who go to the dungeons never come out or see the light of day again.

I weave an easy spell of concealment as I emerge from the staircase into the dungeons.

The air smells moldy and damp. As I soundlessly walk past the cells, the stench of festering wounds and unwashed bodies hits me.

The thought of Amalia being down here makes me so angry I could tear the walls down with my bare fucking hands.

I barely know her, yet I feel as if I've known her my entire life. Like she and Os are...some missing piece I've been searching for. Being around them, either of them or both, gives me hope.

I find Amalia's cell at the very back of the dungeon. Her blood-covered body is curled into a tight ball on the dirty floor. I can sense that she's awake. Drifting in and out of consciousness, but she's here.

"You can stop pretending to be asleep. I know you're awake," I don't mean for my words to come out rude, but I'm worried, and worry so easily turns into something sharper. Instantly I regret my tone.

Even in the safety of our minds, her voice is broken. *"Go away, Nyall."*

It's a physical pain, the hollowness in Amalia's voice. Her fire is gone.

All that's left is sadness.

"You're damn lucky I intercepted the soldier who was on his way to tell my Father about this. Still, we must be quick." I try to motivate her, try to say anything to get her on her feet.

"Leave me here. Let me die."

Fuck.

Memories hit me. Memories of the day Os thinks I betrayed him.

Of the day I realized my father was everything I didn't want to believe. Evil.

I wanted to die that day, and the years that followed. I drowned myself in spirits, though the buzz of alcohol was always short-lived. I numbed the pain with anything I could find.

No one knows that some of my tattoos are to cover the scars. The marks I've left on myself using iron blades, so the cuts will never fully heal.

I will not let Amalia Roth go through that.

"You're coming with me whether you like it or not, horse girl."

She's on her feet before I can take a single breath, her hands dart through the bars of the stall and around my throat.

Oh...my God.

Her fire isn't gone at all. There is no visible flame but Amalia burns with the heat of a newborn star. Her skin vacillates between freezing cold and burning hot.

For the first time in a long time, I fear. Not of her but *for* her.

"Don't. Ever. Call me that again," Amalia hisses aloud, more draconian in this moment than any Dragon I've ever seen.

She drops her hands and pushes away from me with a strangled breath. I can hear her little heart racing.

How I wish I could take this pain from her; though I know I can't. I activate one of the spells inked onto my skin. A spell of transference.

I step through the bars and bend down, wiping the tears off Amalia's face.

"What happened?" Her entire body is trembling. *"Amalia, what the fuck happened? The guards were talking about some girl who snapped and attacked everyone.*

I don't want to tell her what I found. Not yet. This is her story, her trauma.

Whatever she wants to share with me, I accept.

Her tearstained eyes meet mine as Amalia places her hand over mine.

There's a painful pinch in the back of my head as she blasts through my walls. I drop them instantly, allowing her in.

Amalia can't tell me what happened...so she shows me instead. But as she does so, she also lets her emotions bleed into me. I feel her rage, her soul-deep sorrow. I feel the heavy weight of her grief like it's a blanket over my shoulders.

"Oh, Amalia..." I breathe. *"I'm so sorry, sweetheart. I'm so, so fucking sorry."*

Gently, I pick her up, cradling her muscular body against me. She could be covered in shit and guts, and I wouldn't care.

"He loved you, Amalia. Know that. I've watched hate towards animals, and I've watched animals hate. Taran trusted you—a gift of which few people ever are lucky enough to receive." Her tears fall harder

"Go away, Nyall." Her voice is hollow and torn as she looks away from me.

I tug her body closer. *"I'm not leaving you, Amalia."*

Aloud, I issue the gentle command, "Hold your breath, sweetheart."

Using the last dregs of my magyk, I use another spell inked onto my body and teleport us outside. It only works short distances, and it has to be a place I've been, but the fresh air of the garden has never smelled better.

Amalia protests lightly but I ignore it, carrying her through the gardens with a tight grip.

"Why are you doing this, Nyall?" she asks.

~~*Because for some reason I care about you, and I don't know why. Because you deserve better.*~~

Instead, I say, *"Maybe I'm not the monster you want me to be, Amalia. Do I need a reason?"*

"The Fae love to deceive," she coughs.

I sigh and set her down at the top of the staircase to the Dragon Pit.

"Fine, Amalia. You win. I am doing this because every fucking time I look at you, I see the pain in your eyes, and it breaks me because it.." I take a deep breath, "Because it reminds me so much of my own pain. I know what it is to feel alone, Amalia. I know what it is to wonder if there's any point in going forward at all."

She looks away.

"Who knows? Maybe all of this is for nothing, and no difference will be made. Maybe we're not meant to make it out of this, and our time is simply through. But I'm sick of looking into the faces of my people and seeing their misery. I don't care if this kills me, Amalia. But if it gives anyone even the smallest chance of happiness, of hope for the future, then the pain is worth it."

I hold up my black-veined hand. Practicing the old, Elven magyk has come with a price.

"If my death is what it takes to get there, then I welcome it. In that, we are alike."

She's quiet as we walk down the stairs, heading not for the dormitory, but for Os' room.

I'm glad she finds comfort with him, and he with her. They deserve it.

I just...I wish I could experience it too. That happiness.

"He's the bravest male I have ever known. Os, I mean," I don't know why I say it, but now that I've started, I can't stop. *"He's a damn grouch and old as dirt...but he's a good male."*

"I never asked your opinion," Amalia's voice is numb.

We make it to Os' room and Amalia opens the door but there's a blur as Os grabs hold of me and tosses me across the room.

I could have stopped it, but I let it happen. The pain is grounding.

His fist meets my face, shattering my nose as blood coats my tongue.

A pained noise in the background stops us both.

Without thinking, we both blur and appear at Amalia's side, realizing the sound came from her. Os grabs her face, looking over her with fury in his golden gaze. *"A gahrá,* tell me you're okay. Did he hurt you?"

"Did you not see?" Her voice is scratchy.

Remus shakes his head, *"You...blocked me. Don't do that again, A gahrá. Not when you're in pain."*

She...blocked him? *Interesting.* I don't think they're aware that I can hear their mental conversation. I do not mention it, because a part of me feels like I'm eavesdropping.

"Amalia, talk to me. What happened? Why were you in such pain?" I can hear the panic bleed into his voice.

They don't realize that I can hear their thoughts.

"Oh, my Gods, Ama, are you okay? Where have you been? You didn't show up for dinner and I got so worried!" Dyana opens the door from the bathroom to see Amalia standing there. She almost knocks me over as she wraps her friend in a tight hug.

"He's gone," Amalia says numbly.

"What?" Dyana asks, taken aback. "Who is gone, Ama?"

"Taran is gone," Os answers for her.

Dyana's hand flies up to cover her mouth, "What? Oh, Gods."

"They skinned him alive. Tortured him..." Her voice is detached as she replays the events of the day.

At that moment, Mirielle enters, "Dyana, I haven't seen her anywhere—oh good, you're back." Mirielle pauses, laughing nervously, "Why does everyone look like someone died?"

I almost cringe at the bad timing of the joke, not that it's Mirielle's fault.

Dyana quietly explains and everyone goes silent for a while, processing the loss.

"It's enough," Amalia says with a tone of finality.

"It's enough," Amalia repeats, facing me. "I will help you, on one condition."

Nyall looks at me, oddly serious. "Of course. Name it."

"Your father's life is mine. It will be my swords he falls upon, my eyes he sees when he takes his last breath. He is mine."

Of all the things she could ask...

That is the one thing I cannot give.

"You forget yourself, Arkaydian. Achan's life is mine to take." I watch the fury rise in her eyes. "But...I'm always willing to share. When the time comes, we will be the ones to finish it. If that works for you—"

"Done."

I blink. How easily she agreed.

"If Amalia is in," Os grumbles, "then I am as well. But test me, Prince, and I'll clean my teeth with your bones."

Holy shit.

Holy shit.

Never in my wildest dreams did I think Amalia would accept, let alone Os.

I just wish it wasn't for such a horrible reason.

"Well," I drawl. "Welcome to the Rebellion, then."

"I wasn't done," Amalia stops me. "I need one more favor."

"This can't be good," I mutter.

"Listen, you want our help, this is what we need. We're putting our lives on the line for you, Prince. The least you could do is listen."

She's right, which is why I nod as such. "What is it?"

"I recognize that you must have some long set plan in place," I start. "But that plan will have to change, because we're going to free the Dragons." Dyana, Mirielle, and Nyall all turn to look at me, eyes wide. "All of them."

God. *I want to marry her.*

The thought hits me so hard I nearly stumble. I conceal my surprise with a light cough but Os watches me with keen eyes, missing nothing.

Does he know that I like her? Does it even matter?

I...I *do* like her. I haven't let myself admit it until now. Not truly. But watching as someone so full of grief and sorrow can turn that into motivation for *good*...it's spellbinding.

"How are we supposedly doing this?" I ask, rubbing my temples. They will think I'm doing this out of frustration, but really, it's my head. The higher Elven magyks are draining me and I haven't slept in days. The dull throbbing at my temples is getting stronger by the minute.

Amalia and Os have a silent conversation before the former turns to me and says, "I bring a message. From the Crimson Queen."

We all go still. "She said the answer you're looking for lies with Lazarus. No clue what it means, but I'm assuming you do."

Goddamnit.

How could I have missed it?

The Lazarus Construct is an ancient Elven spell for transference. I have spent centuries building my siphoning spell and perfecting it, but there was always something missing.

I'm a fucking *idiot.* The base of the spell needs to be the shape of the Lazarus construct. Of course.

"Well, I guess we're saving all of the Dragons in a week," I laugh.

Mirielle balks, "Nyall, you can't be serious!"

Dyana glares at her.

Amalia clucks her tongue in disappointment, "Who's the coward now?"

Mir's light eyes flare in anger as her cheeks flush. Dyana looks pissed at Amalia for saying anything at all.

"You're damn right I'm serious. It's the perfect distraction. Everyone in the entire city will be packed into the Arena, and all of their eyes will be on the Gauntlet."

"It's suicide. Now you'll only help if we pull off something impossible?" Mirielle sputters.

"Look around, Mirielle. This has always been a suicide mission. You wanted to be a hero. You wanted to make a difference. Well, here it is. Here's your chance. Suck it up and be the hero."

I want to defend Mirielle, but I also know Amalia is right.

"Fine, but if this was a foolhardy plan before, it's even more impossible now. But yeah, fine. Let's go free the freaking Dragons," Mirielle says, her tone one of disbelief and frustration.

Dyana is the first one to speak up, but she speaks only to Amalia.

"If we do this, there's no going back."

Amalia gives her a sad, hollow smile, "I know."

"I need to do this. I've sat in the shadows long enough, Dy. I accept the consequences of this choice."

Dyana blinks tears away but nods, trusting her friend.

"But Dy? Look at me." Amalia walks over and grabs Dyana's arms gently. "You don't have to help us. I told you, I'll always keep you safe. I won't be mad if you don't want to be involved. The choice is your own."

"Of course, I'm helping, you idiot. Can't let you go off on your own now, can I? Who would break up all the fights you *'accidentally'* start when you look at someone the wrong way?" She sniffles, pulling away from me with laughter in her eyes.

"I will guard her, Amalia. Nothing will get past me." Mirielle suddenly stands next to them, her gray eyes fierce.

"Fine. Now can somebody just freaking tell me how in the actual four Hells were going to save all of the Dragons?" Dyana forces her voice to sound brave, but I can feel the fear emanating from her.

There are many good reasons to be afraid of what we're about to do.

CHAPTER 32
OS

How do you tell someone you love them when you're both about to die?

Amalia Roth came into my life when I least expected it, but now I can't imagine my days without her.

I don't *want* to imagine spending my days without her.

Ever since the day she found Taran, she's been different. She's slept over almost nightly since that dreaded day at the barn, and every night, she wakes us both with her screams.

Her nightmares are getting worse. Something I'm all too familiar with. Exhaustion lines her face, accenting her pale eyes with dark purple circles beneath them.

The plan we decided on is foolhardy. There is a very real chance it won't work. But we've all lived and *lost*. At some point, the grief must stop. It has to.

"Come here," I whisper, picking her up from my bed. Tearstains coat her cheeks. "Let's get you clean."

"I'm fine," she mumbles, but we both know that's a lie.

"You're not fine, and that's okay."

Amalia sighs, cuddling closer to my chest, my tunic held tightly in her pale, freckled hands.

I carry her into the bathing room and set her down on the edge of the tub. I don't usually bathe with the tub—I prefer to stand—but right now, I just want to hold her.

The bath fills with steaming water and I dump in some lavender-scented soap before helping Amalia strip out of her clothes.

I suffocate my rising desire. Right now, sex isn't on my mind. Making sure Amalia is okay is all that matters to me.

She protests every step of the way, and every step of the way, I don't listen.

I know what it's like to go your whole life without anyone to take care of you.

I sink into the tub behind her, pulling her tight against my chest. My arms easily go around her soft waist as we settle into the hot water.

We sit like that in silence for a while. Long enough that I have to refill the tub with more hot water.

"Tilt your head back," I whisper, pressing a gentle kiss to her lithe neck. "Let me wash you."

"I don't—"

"Shh," I murmur. "Let me do this, *A gahrá.* Please."

She sighs and I feel her body slowly relax in my arms. I grab a bar of soap from the edge of the tub and work it into a rich lather. One by one, I massage her hands and arms, moving up to her shoulders and neck.

"Ow," she groans as I work on a big knot at the base of her skull.

"Would you like me to stop?" I ask, reducing the pressure of my touch.

Her hand grips my arm a second later and I find her blue eyes gazing back at me.

"Please...don't stop."

I caress her cheek and press a kiss against her forehead. "Then I won't. Just close your eyes and try to relax."

"Easier said than done," she sighs, but eventually, the knots in her back and neck give way, softening and relaxing.

"There you go," I breathe. "Just like that."

I turn her gently, moving on to her legs and feet. Knots line her calves, and I carefully work those out as well, making sure not to hurt her.

Soon, she's squeaky clean.

I turn her once more and tilt her head back, dunking her hair into the water as I massage soap into it.

She lets out a pleased moan. Amalia loves when I play with her hair.

When the soap is rinsed out, I rub some solid oils in the ends to make it soft.

"Where did you get that?" she asks, her voice sleepy.

"This?" I ask, showing her the oil. "Dragons are vain creatures, *A gahrá*. Maybe I like how it makes my hair look."

Amalia snorts.

"Or," I begin rinsing the ends of her hair, "perhaps I was waiting for this moment and I saved it just for you."

I *feel* rather than see her blush.

"Kiss-ass," she murmurs, but feeling the happiness it brings her is unmatched.

Once her hair is rinsed, I lather my hands and soap up her breasts. I tug lightly at her hard nipples, making her moan and wiggle. Reaching beneath the surface of the water, I rinse the soap from my hands before dragging my fingers along the seam of her legs.

Amalia gasps, leaning even harder into me as her body relaxes further.

"Relax, *A gahrá.*"

I press one finger inside of her, massaging her inner walls. She's so tight and warm, I never want to leave.

OURS. SHE IS OURS! My Beast roars his pleasure.

Not ours. MINE.

Long ago, before my true form was locked away, my thoughts were singular. I was one being; Dragon and male. The centuries of separation also separated our thoughts, our being.

I started to hear my Dragon's thoughts, whereas before, there was no line between us.

This is the first time I've felt our thoughts merge in...a very long time.

A low, vibration begins rattling in my chest.

Akin to a cat's purr, Dragons rattle when they're pleased.

My familiar is *healing* me. The distance between male and Dragon is once again, growing shorter. We are one and the same as I am with Amalia.

She lets out a mewing cry as I add another finger, slowly fucking her with my hand. She turns her head, hiding in my chest and I wrap my spare arm around her, tucking her tight against me.

"I like that sound," she gasps, but it ends on a moan as I hit that perfect spot.

"And I like *that* sound."

She pants harder, wiggling against me as her hips thrust, dislodging and splashing the water out of the tub; but I couldn't care less.

"Come for me, *A gahrá.* Come on my hand."

Amalia lets out a loud moan as her walls tighten around me and the orgasm rocks through her.

I never stop the gentle thrusting. I ride out the wave of Amalia's pleasure as I hold her in my arms.

I don't know what I expect, but I don't expect her to cry.

"I'm—sorry," she gasps as the sobs wreck her.

"Don't you *dare* apologize," I snarl, holding her tightly. I gently tilt her face towards me, looking into her watery, gorgeous eyes. "There is *nothing* you need to be ashamed of and there is *nothing* you could ever do that would push me away."

Amalia's eyes close as she cries harder.

"I'm scared," she whines. I feel the panic in her voice.

"I am too," I admit quietly. "Fucking terrified."

I go quiet as Amalia's tears coat my damp chest.

"It's okay to be scared," I whisper. "We fear because we love."

"Love hurts," she hiccups. "I don't want it. I don't want to feel this way. Constantly afraid and hurting. Somedays I-I can't even breathe, Remus. It's like a giant stone is sitting on my chest and I can't inhale because the grief is so heavy."

It kills me that she knows the feeling.

"Look at me," I whisper. Her tearstained face meets my gaze. "You are stronger because you love. It's the difference between us and them. They don't love or even understand what it means to care."

Amalia nods and I feel the exhaustion seeping in.

"Come on," I press another kiss against her forehead. "Let's get dry and get into bed. I'll add some more logs to the fire. You need your rest before the Semi-Finals."

In one fell swoop, I pick her up and stand up from the tub, water dripping down from our bodies.

Wrapping her in a thick towel, I dry her off and braid her hair before tucking her into bed and crawling in behind her.

"Thank you," she whispers into the dark. The crackling fireplace is the only light left in the room.

"I am yours, A gahrá. There is nothing to thank me for."

She's quiet for a moment before turning to face me. She tucks in beneath my chin, wrapping her strong arms around me.

"And I...am yours," Amalia whispers.

Pleasure flows through me and my chest starts to vibrate. We fall asleep like that, curled together, pretending the outside world doesn't exist.

I am terrified, because for the first time in a very long time, I have something to *lose.*

CHAPTER 33

OS

Fae, Demis, and Magyka alike are packed into the dusty Arena stands. The overcast winter weather is surprisingly tepid, but we're protected from much of the wind anyway.

The rows of seats are packed, with no empty space to be seen.

The crowd curses and shouts, screaming as Mirelle and Amalia walk onto the Arena sand.

But I'm not in the Arena; I'm *beneath* it.

"We're in position." Amalia announces in my head. I feel the way she's connecting all of us so we can communicate. I can see the faint lights of the other's minds.

"Dyana, are you ready?"

I hold up a hand, stopping Dyana from going into the light. There are more guards down here than there should be.

"Uh, hold on," Dyana says.

"What's wrong?" I can hear my familiar's panic.

"60 seconds away from the guard rotation." I share, cracking the stiff muscles in my neck.

I have my own plan if the guards don't leave like the Prince promised they would.

"Uh, Nyall? What the fuck is he talking about?" Mirielle says suddenly.

"I don't know—fuck, the Council's minds are blocked. Something's wrong." At Nyall's anxious, vicious words, something settles deep within me.

I knew something was going to go wrong. There's almost a comfort in knowing we're going to get it over with.

"What's going on?" I demand.

"I don't know. Achan has some godsdamn surprise for us, which is never good news."

"Now," I say out loud. The guards begin to leave, and we sneak into the light, but as we turn the corner to the Crimson Queen's stall, we run into a group of guards.

Lovely.

They have no time to scream before I blur and rip their heads off with my bare hands.

Dyana's eyes are wide and her mouth hanging open as she watches me. The ground goes from clean to covered in blood in seconds.

"MOVE!" I shout at her, and we run to the Queen's stall...but it's empty.

Fuck.

"We have a serious fucking problem," Amalia snarls, but I already know what she's going to say.

"Nothing else matters on the sand, A gahrá. Nothing." I remind her. She has to stay alive.

She must.

Nyall cuts in, *"Achan knows something. She wasn't the Dragon originally picked for this event. I checked this morning, and another was listed. What the fuck happened?"* Now it's his turn to pause and let out expletives. He snarls, sounding more Dragon than me. *"Amalia, Os is right. You cannot care about her now. Nothing else matters but making sure you live long enough to finish through on the plan. In 15 seconds, you need to move. The distraction has to happen. You cannot hesitate."*

Kydis is her opponent...and now the one thing standing in the way of our survival.

"A gahrá...I'm so sorry." I whisper the words only to Amalia.

"We proceed as planned," her voice is shaky. *"And I'm breaking that godsdamn compulsion."*

Then our connection goes silent.

"I can't hear them," Dyana says frantically.

Fuck this.

"Open the stalls!" I shout at Dyana and begin doing the same.

"What about the spell?" Dyana asks, which is when guards turn the corner.

"GO!"

Dyana nods and begins unlocking stalls, trying her hardest to push them open. The Dragons help, using their weak claws and snouts to nudge the doors open wide enough for them to get through.

"THEY'RE ESCAPING!" a guard shouts, but his words are cut off in a gurgle as I punch my fist down his throat and rip out his spinal cord.

The anger overwhelms me, and I lose myself in the bloodlust.

My Dragon is itching to burst out and I use that momentum, that innate *magyk*, to break into Amalia's head. I know it probably hurt but we can't stop now.

"Amalia, can you hear me?" I ask in her head as Guards swarm me. I'm keeping their attention off of Dyana while she runs through the aisles.

Just then, a loud cry comes from the ceiling and something big thumps to the ground.

Then something smaller.

I turn, tossing the guards off my back and shattering bones as I smack their bodies down to the floor.

The Dragonguard.

I don't want to kill it, but the larger of the two attacks me. The Dragon is a green, a dark, deep green, almost black, with bright red-orange eyes.

"I'm sorry," I whisper before shifting my nails and weaving, avoiding its sharp jaws. "I'm so sorry," I repeat the words as I drag my claws across the sensitive, delicate emerald scales of its belly.

The Dragon had no chance.

It cries out in pain, crashing into the metal stalls so hard, it breaks open its nose.

The smaller Dragon, a white, cowers beneath me. It runs away, knowing it can't win this fight.

For a moment, I consider chasing and killing it.

But the Dragonguard cannot help their situation. They've been bred to obey, manipulated before they even hatched from their eggs.

"Trigger the damned spell! We can't wait any longer!" I shout at Amalia, kicking the green Dragon's limp carcass into an empty stall.

"Uh Ama, your boyfriend killed some people...er, uh, a lot of people actually...and some of the Dragonguard..." Dyana says casually.

"DO IT NOW!" My scream is desperate.

There's a brief pause before I feel magyk shooting into the ground, all the way down to the Pit. It's like an electric shock. With a loud *clank* all of the stalls open, freeing every single Dragon.

"It worked. Holy shit, it worked. Amalia, the spell worked. The stalls are open." Dyana shrieks, the volume of her mental voice so loud it makes my ears ring.

The large silver Dragon—Vesimyr—approaches immediately.

"They took her," his voice is a deep bellow in my mind. ***"They took Kydis. They took our QUEEN!"***

I nod sadly as more guards swarm us.

With a snarl so terrifying, it makes my heart skip a beat, Vesimyr whips his thick tail out and slams the guards into the wall, crushing them completely.

When his tail pulls away, there's only battered, smushed piles of flesh.

"DRAGONS! OUR FREEDOM IS AT HAND. DIG LIKE YOUR LIFE DEPENDS ON IT!" Even I flinch at the power in Vesimyr's voice as he projects the words to all Dragons in the near vicinity.

The answering roars make tears pool in the corners of my eyes.

"You," Vesimyr looks at Dyana and she jumps. ***"Get on."***

"WHAT?" Dyana screams, but our time is short. With a growl I run over to her, grab her around the waist, and toss her at the silver Dragon.

Vesimyr catches the screaming mortal in his claws, depositing her on his back. She quickly rights herself, holding onto the sharp spikes along his spine.

Cracking his neck, Vesimyr raises his wings and flies up to the ceiling. Many of the others cannot fly, but what the scrolls never mentioned is that Dragons can *climb*. Our sharp nails make it easy.

"GRAB THE HATCHLINGS!" I call, and an emerald Dragon, small in size but no less fierce, nods. She disappears before returning with wiggling bundles of fabric carrying eggs and small hatchlings. Several of the Dragons follow suit before they all begin climbing up the walls.

"BEASTKYN! SHIFT AND GET UP HERE. I NEED YOUR CLAWS."

"THIS IS VERY SCARY!" Dyana's shout follows. "I WANT YOU ALL TO KNOW THAT!"

"Hold on, mortal. Hold on tight." Vesimyr says, his voice calmer and lower.

Shift.

I have to—shift. I *can* shift.

I haven't dared think about it since the moment Amalia broke the spell that locked me within this form. But I've felt it. Felt *me.* The real me.

It's like a missing piece of myself has returned. With scream, I let my head fall back as my Beast rips through my human skin.

Every bone, every muscle, every blood cell; everything changes. Exploding with the kind of divinity only a Dragon can understand.

Scales burst through my skin as flesh falls to the floor, peeling away from my mortal bones as they too begin to shift.

The ground gets farther and farther away as my body grows. Legs and hands turn into claws.

Wings burst from my back. Giant, pristine black wings. The Dragons climbing above turn to look, their eyes wide.

I am...*whole.* And I'm going to save my familiar, even if it kills me.

"Nyall? Can you hear this?" I ask as I flare my wings, flapping them lightly. The movement is both foreign and familiar. But this is not the time to hesitate.

I burn through the fear in my belly and let out another roar, jumping into the air as my wings carry me to the ceiling.

I'm flying.

I'm fucking *flying.*

"Yes," Nyall says. *"I can hear you, Os. You feel...different."*

"Drop the barrier. The stalls are open, and the Dragons are beginning to dig. Now is the time for that distraction!"

"Oh good, now the real fun begins," the Prince chuckles and I *feel* the violence and anger within him.

In this moment, I realize that Nyall Drayven really does hate his father.

The Prince triggers the barrier ward he wove onto the Arena stands this morning. The ward bounces into existence, invisible to all but blocking all outside magic from being felt.

Whatever happens outside of the Arena—or beneath it—won't be heard.

"I'm beginning the Siphon weaving. At my signal, disarm Achan." Nyall replies, and everything goes quiet in my head as my thoughts shut off. Nyall just made the entire arena into a void field. No telepathy or psychic magyks.

"Whatever you're planning? Make it good." Amalia snarls.

I push to the front of the tunnel and the other Dragons bow their heads in deference.

I can't stop to think about it. Can't hesitate and linger on the fact that the kin who shunned me for years are now bowing to me.

There is only her. I have to get to Amalia.

Dyana is crouched down on Vesimyr's back, her hair covered in dust and dirt. She coughs but holds on.

"We'll get to her," I whisper in her mind as I join Vesimyr, digging my nails into the ground as we tunnel up towards the Arena.

The Dragons who are able to join us, but Vesimyr and I head the charge.

Dragons have an innate ability to sense the suns and moons. We can tell how far underground we are. Slowly, too slowly, we ascend towards the Arena.

Noise suddenly bursts into my head.

The ward is down.

"Why the fuck is the ward down?" I shout at Nyall.

"Hurry. You have to hurry. I don't—" the Prince pauses. *"Oh shit. Oh shit."*

"What the hell is happening? We're almost there!"

"Amalia...she knocked out Kydis & Mirielle. She's...she's revealing herself."

Fear floods my heart, but I'm not surprised. Amalia isn't a bad person. Her problem is she loves too hard.

She would do anything to protect those she cares about...including sacrifice herself.

I know what she is. I know she is more than just an Arkaydian. I have always known. The second I tasted her blood; I knew Amalia Roth wasn't her real name.

In the dark of the night, as we laid together in bed, she told me her story.

Her *real* story, and her *real* name.

"HURRY!" I shout at Vesimyr. We dig faster and faster, just nearing the surface when a giant BOOM makes dust fall from the ceiling. The Dragons shriek but we don't stop.

We're almost at the surface, close enough that I can hear Amalia's voice projected in the distance amidst the screams of terror from the Arena audience.

"I am the Right Hand of the Morrigyn, and you, Achan Drayven, have been found *guilty*."

There's a moment of pause before a loud scream reaches us.

Then the ground begins to shake.

Nyall has been laying the symbols for weeks now, all in hopes that we would make this plan work. His siphon spell is almost primed.

*"Finish the spell. **NOW!**"* Amalia screams in our heads just before everything explodes, and we're all knocked to our backs. The entire back half of the arena collapses, caving into a giant hole as the ground opens up.

I burst through the hole, shoving my huge, Dragon body through the tight space. A huge cloud of dust covers me, and I shake it off before looking down at Achan Drayven and letting out a bloodcurdling **ROAR.**

Despite it all, Amalia Asteroth takes one look at my true form, and she *smiles*.

Vesimyr lets out a mighty screech as he bursts into the Arena, extending his wings—

Wait. *Two* sets of wings. Something tugs at the back of my memories. A story...a legend, even. Of the Dragon with *four* wings. But now isn't the time.

"HURRY!" Dyana screams, yanking me back into the present. "Get on the fucking Dragon, people!"

"Go!" Amalia shouts at Mirielle.

"What about Nyall?" the redhead responds, but there's no time. A beam of magyk heads their way. Amalia shoves her forward, throwing up her arm and creating a shield of pure Hellfyre to shield the two of them.

The navy-blue flames *simmer* as they take the brunt of the magykal attack.

The Archmage and his sycophants appear out of thin air, their gray robes dragging along the dirt floor. More Fae guards shout and run in now that they can see us.

Then I see him.

Achan Drayven. In the flesh.

KILL HIM. FEAST ON HIS FLESH. I open my jaw and let out a roar so loud, Amalia and Mirielle hit the ground. Achan and the Archmage disappear, reappearing to the side as the latter raises a hand and shoots a beam of purple magyk at me. It hits me in the chest, and I'm slammed to the ground, scales singed and burning.

Amalia snarls, lowering her Hellfyre shield. Guards swarm me but I lash out with a roar, tearing through their bodies with my sharp claws.

Blood sprays and it tastes delicious on my tongue, despite the rotten flavor of Fae meat.

"Amalia!" Mirielle shouts. "The Archmage can't get Nyall. The spell can't stop!"

"Come on, get on!" Dyana screams, and I'm caught. I want to help Amalia, I want to help Nyall, but I also want Dyana to get out of here alive.

Fuck.

"The dark magyk is killing you, you fucking idiot. You're going to send the entire kingdom to the bottom of the ocean if you don't stop!" Nyall shouts at Achan, throwing a spell made of white light that turns into spikes that rain down on Achan, who cries out and tries to shield unsuccessfully. "Then what comes next, Father? When you've destroyed everything in this world, what's next? Will you go to another world and do the same thing, never satisfied with the power you were born with? Why is it never enough for you?" The magyk bursts towards Achan's shield and begins planting hooks in him. Nyall yanks both of his hands, and dark red magyk begins to stream out as Nyall starts siphoning his father.

"Go, Mirielle! Get Dyana out of here!" I scream at Mirielle. There's no other choice. I curse and sprint towards the huge steel-colored Dragon still lying down, awaiting the rest of its passengers.

Mirielle takes a great running leap, and easily jumps on the Dragon's back, mounting just behind Dyana.

"Amalia, come on! We need to go!" Dyana cries, but I know the truth.

I've known the whole time.

What she would do to save them. To save all of us. It's what I've been so afraid of.

Amalia never planned on surviving.

"Vesimyr, get them out of here." A voice so powerful and ancient, it's a physical weight on my spine sounds in our minds.

Kydis.

The Crimson Queen. Her dark red scales are bloody and ripped up.

"Keep them safe. You know what to do."

"Yes, my Queen." Vesimyr responds. He lets out a mighty screech and the Dragons begin to climb.

Most sport terrible old injuries, their wings torn and filled with holes, fangs broken, bodies worn and weary.

But their eyes all glow as freedom sits just on the horizon. The first Dragons begin taking flight, unsteady, but the sky is theirs. It knows them. Soon, dozens get into the air, some holding bundles of wiggling fabric containing the hatchlings.

I want to sob with joy, if it weren't for the fear still holding my heart within its grasp.

"Wait, no! We need to go back! Amalia!" Dyana starts screaming as she realizes what's going on. Mirielle holds her tightly as Vesimyr begins climbing out of the Arena.

Guards surround Amalia, but she unleashes more Hellfyre, turning them to ash.

Nyall unleashes another Magykal assault on his Father. Though there's someone missing—

The Archmage appears next to me, with Mirielle's staff in his hands.

He moves quickly, far too quickly for a Fae or Elf, and stabs the staff through my chest.

The pain throws me off. I let out a loud roar and feel my hold on my Dragon form slip from my grasp. Back in mortal form, I grab hold of the staff and yank it out with a shout. Blood sprays everywhere.

Too much blood. Long ago, my body healed fast. So fast, you could watch my scales and skin reknit themselves.

Now my power is dimmed.

I will not heal in time. With a deep breath, I summon my flame and spit fire onto the wound, cauterizing it.

The blood continues to flow.

The Archmage is at my back a second later. I weave, avoiding the blow from his glowing purple magyk, but I stumble from the blood loss.

From the corner of my eye, I watch as Amalia screams and charges Achan Drayven, only to get thrown into the air with a vicious bolt of magyk. She just gets up and charges again, over and over, still screaming with such gut-wrenching pain.

Nyall sneaks up behind Achan and continues siphoning. The black veins on his hands get darker and more visible as Achan cries out and falls to his knees, gasping for air as his skin begins to crack like dry paper. But the Archmage appears next to Nyall, blasting him with a spell that almost ruins the siphoning completely. Achan is momentarily safe but Amalia charges, letting out a roar of pure rage and shooting him with a blast of Hellfyre.

When she's done, she pants as the Hellfyre disperses. But there stands Achan Drayven; still alive.

Still alive.

Something isn't right.

Nyall yells, roaring to the Gods in the Heavens as the siphon spell dies within his hands, the ribbons of white light he's been weaving dying out completely.

It didn't work.

Our plan didn't work.

The Arena is empty. The other Dragons have been crawling out, some with small bundles in their talons. The babies.

Kydis growls, prowling towards us. The Archmage steps away from me, moving closer to Achan.

But the Archmage just smiles, purple eyes amused as he snaps his fingers, and one of the baby Dragons appears at Achan Drayven's feet, a little red one with copper eyes. The hatchling sits up, its small wings thin and light pink.

My heart stops.

Kydis jerks back, trembling with fury. Amalia's knees hit the sand, her eyes wide.

It's the *Queen's* hatchling.

"Submit, or I will kill your child," Drayven says simply.

"Go, Vesimyr! Get out of here!" Kydis roars. ***"Get our people home."***

Amalia's eyes glow as she falls to her knees, looking upon the hatchling.

"You will not hurt my child." A booming voice echoes throughout the ruins of the arena. Kydis never opened her mouth, but the voice is clearly her. She sounds old, but the power in her words makes my skin feel like it's peeling right off my bones.

"Hello, Dragon. See something you want?" Achan Drayven sneers.

I stumble over to Amalia, trying to get to her. But Amalia's attention isn't on me...

It's on the sky.

We all watch in horror as the Archmage sends a magyk arrow up into the sky—right into Dyana Arkos. Dyana takes a final, gasping breath before slumping against Mirielle as they disappear into the clouds on the back of the silver Dragon.

Dyana's dead.

I never see the second arrow.

Not until it's too late.

My eyes meet Amalia's as the world slows down.

"You should've come with me, little Asteroth. Now you're all alone again, no help and no one to save you but me," Achan smiles, blood smeared over his face as he appears in front of her. His words begin to sound fuzzy and distant.

"Your God is a fraud, and you are a blight upon this world," a deep voice booms. Kydis approaches from behind Amalia, stepping over her as she lets out a mighty roar and pounces on Achan Drayven and the Archmage.

They simply sidestep, but Achan uses the moment to jump onto Kydis' back.

I fall to the ground as Achan abandons the red hatchling. It squeaks, scared.

Kydis' eyes shut in pain as Achan stabs her in the back with a dagger. Then her eyes open, and she looks right at Amalia, **"The Left Hand protects, and the Right punishes. Balance the scales, Amalia Asteroth. Become who you were born to be."**

Everything goes sharp as I groan, lifting my head to look at Amalia.

There is so much I want to say, but not enough time.

"You are everything I have ever wanted... Thank you for showing me one last slice of happiness; thank you for making me remember what it is to fly."

"Keep her safe, Daughter of Shadow," Kydis roars aloud and a bright red burst of magyk explodes from her, then a weight is falling on my chest.

The hatchling squeaks in fear, wiggling violently as Amalia picks it up, cradling the young Dragon to her chest,

"Keep her safe."

Those are her final words as Achan stabs Kydis in the back again and she screams in pain.

Magyk hits me in a wave so strong, I nearly choke on it.

Amalia's trying to heal me. But because we didn't complete the bond it...it won't work.

Across the sand, Nyall Drayven catches my eye.

His white hair is soaked in blood, and he pants, exhausted. But I'm surprised to see my own rage mirrored in his mismatched gaze. Then he looks at the blood dripping from my wounds and the arrow still sticking out of my chest.

"Do it," I groan in his head. *"KILL HIM!"*

Kydis extends her wings and takes to the air, a complete vertical ascent, something a much younger Dragon would never be able to do. Achan Drayven is yanked into the air, shouting and blasting her with bolt after bolt of magyk in an attempt to get her back on the ground.

The Archmage however does nothing. He just glances at them before disappearing, leaving Achan to his fate.

Achan hangs on for dear life as he continues battering away at Kydis, her scales burning right off her body. Nyall sprints across the sand towards Amalia, a spell beginning to flare to life within his hands.

The magyk building with me explodes out in a wave of heat and ice so intense the stone of the Arena begins to melt and break. The entire building shudders and begins collapsing on itself.

In the sky, Kydis disappears into the clouds.

Then she reappears, only this time, she's heading straight for the ground at full speed.

A death fall; one she will not recover from.

Kydis shoots toward the ground, a brightly burning red star who now clutches Achan Drayven within her talons.

It's the silence that follows as we watch her spear toward the ground, Achan Drayven screaming in her hold. He stabs at her legs, trying to break free.

The world starts to go blurry, and stars burst behind my vision as I watch Amalia use a beam of Hellfyre to hold Achan's body on Kydis' back, preventing any escape.

Nyall does the same, white ribbons of light shooting off him to wrap around Achan, holding him in place.

Through my blurred vision, I watch as Kydis, the Crimson Queen, completes her death dive, taking Achan Drayven with her.

When they land, the weight is so immense that it finishes the job I started. The ground cracks and begins to cave in as the Arena starts disappearing into the Dragon Pit, collapsing into the earth.

Amalia meets my gaze and the world stops.

Then I see Nyall Drayven's mismatched gaze.

"Take care of her," I gasp in his head. *"Please."*

"Os, I—"

"PROMISE ME!"

I hear Nyall's sob in my thoughts, and it makes my heart weep.

"I promise."

The world disappears as Amalia and Nyall's faces fade and there is only *darkness.*

CHAPTER 34
NYALL

We land hard, my ribs protesting the hard ground. The smell of frozen forest tells me where we are.

"No, take me back," Amalia cries. "Take me back!"

I let go of Amalia and get up, trying to figure out if we need to find safety. We're in some large cave that looks to be semi-inhabited but abandoned.

As if someone lived here long ago.

I look at Amalia as she lays prone on the cold stone floor, quiet sobs wrecking her body. The red hatchling crawls on top of her, seeking warmth.

It's terrified.

"Amalia...I can't take you back," I say gently, walking back over to her. I crouch down, kneeling on the ground before her.

"I DON'T CARE! TAKE ME BACK!" she screams, shoving at my chest. She slaps and punches and hits until there's nothing left, her body collapsing in my arms. "Take me back," she sobs.

Howls sound from outside. My magyk is depleted, but I grab two wickedly sharp daggers anyways.

"Please," she sobs, her voice low and scratchy. "Please take me back."

I can't reply, because she and I already know the truth.

There is no going back from this. No matter how much it hurts.

The sudden stampede of dozens upon dozens of heavy, thick paws as giant Dyre Wolves appear at the entrance of the cave.

"Holy shit," I curse as the pack of Dyre Wolves descend on the cave. "Amalia, I don't think this is a good—"

The largest Dyre Wolf—a huge, black beast with thick fur—pushes past me and shoves his nose against Amalia's cheek, licking her.

"Ah. I see you know each other."

This...is Amalia's *family*.

"They're all dead. They...they're all dead," she cries to the wolf, and the wolf cries back.

Full-body sobs explode as she shatters completely, crying so hard it eventually turns into screams. The wolf whines, echoing her pain. The rest of the pack whines and cries, tails between their legs as they crowd around, each pressing their bodies against her. I end up shoved between tails and fluffy heads.

"Take me back," Amalia begs. "Please, take me back."

I gently reach around and cradle Amalia against me. Virgyl growls lightly but lays back down, his eyes never leaving us. I tuck Amalia and the hatchling into my arms as the pack surrounds us, using their furry bodies to absorb our grief. Tears began to fall from my own eyes as I silently grieved the father I should have had, but which Achan Drayven never was.

Amalia turns to look at me, her eyes bloodshot and swollen.

"I'm so sorry, Amalia. I'm so fucking sorry," I whisper, emotion clogging my throat. "You were right. It didn't work. We failed."

A small mind touches mine as we lay there.

"Are you mama?" a small voice asks in our heads, staring at Amalia. A glance beneath the hatchling's belly shows me it's a girl.

"Papa?" The hatchling's voice rings like a bell as she turns her head and looks at me with wide, copper and silver tinged eyes.

She's beautiful.

"She's not your mother, little one. Your mom was so brave, and she loved you so much," I whisper gently, tracing my fingers along her soft scales. *"And I am not your papa."*

"Then who are you?" the little hatchling asks, her voice like twinkling bells.

I go to answer, but someone else answers for me.

"We are friends, and friends are family. You are our family now, little one, you are safe."

The black wolf's voice is powerful yet gentle. The Alpha of the Dyre Wolves.

"What is your name, sweetling?" I ask, caressing my magyk against hers. Amalia cries harder at the gesture.

"I don't...I don't know...but one of the big ones called me Ryu."

Memories of the first time I met Os, and his hatchlings hits me.

He's gone. Os is *gone.* Tears start streaming down my cheeks anew as emotion grips me within its cruel grasp.

"It's nice to meet you, Ryu," I lean forward and press a kiss against the hatchling's snout. She licks me happily. I press a kiss against Amalia's forehead as well, pulling her even tighter against me. I curl my body around hers as exhaustion tugs at both of us.

"I'm going to protect you, Ryu. I'm going to protect you both."

Hours fade into days and days fade into weeks as Amalia Asteroth falls into a deep, dark sleep.

All I can think about are the gold eyes I'll never see again, and the promise I made.

A promise I intend to *keep*.

"How frozen I became
and powerless then,

Ask it not, reader,
for I write it not,
Because all language
would be insufficient.

I did not die, and
I alive remained not."

— Dante Alighieri, 1265-1321.
The Divine Comedy: Inferno

PART THREE:
THE BROKEN

CHAPTER 35
NYALL

Year 500 PBM (3 months since the Arena Collapse)

"NO! PLEASE DON'T LEAVE ME!"

Amalia's screams wake me. Some of the wolves begin whining, scared at the sound. Little Ryu makes a small squeak as it wakes her too. She crawls over to Amalia on all fours, burrowing under the covers to sleep at her belly.

"It's just a dream," I whisper. "Just a dream, sweetheart."

Amalia wakes, her eyes wide and full of terror.

Tears stream down her face, drying on her cheeks. I wrap my body around hers, tucking her and Ryu close against me.

Amalia's pale blue eyes glow in the dark.

"They always leave," she whispers into the midnight shadows.

She feels safe in the dark. I learned this quickly. There's a safety she feels when cradled in shadow. A shield that can allow her to give a voice to the things too difficult to say in the light of day.

"I won't, Amalia. I'm not leaving."

She goes quiet for a while. So quiet, I thought she fell back asleep, until her scratchy voice sounds through the darkness.

"You will."

CHAPTER 36
NYALL

Year 500 PBM (4 months since the Arena Collapse)

"Come on, darling. Use your flames."

"I-I don't know how," Ryu responds. Her voice sounds the same as it did when we first met. She's barely grown since then, but Virgyl told us it's time for her to learn how to control her flames.

Amalia sits beside me, the wet forest floor soaking into her pants. Not much gets a rise out of her these days. The numbness is so thick, I'm not sure she'll ever crawl out of it. I will do anything, *anything* to see the light return to her eyes.

So, I pretend not to grieve. When I think of Os and want to rip the trees from the ground with the depth of my rage, I carve into the mountain instead. Amalia has been the strong one for so long; it's time someone else be strong for her. But I can feel the claws of grief tearing into my soul, draining me, turning me into something full of hate.

"Try again, Ry. It's okay," Amalia whispers, snapping out of it for a moment.

Ryu is her clarity. I thank the fates we were able to save the hatchling. She's become our raft in a tide of stormy seas. The hatchling wrinkles her snout, concentrating hard, when the scales of her bright red belly begin to glow.

Ryu's silver and copper eyes widen and she sneezes, unleashing a tiny, baby, fireball.

"Good job," Amalia smiles—but her eyes remain hollow. "I'm so proud of you."

"As am I," I pick up Ryu and spin her around, making the hatchling shriek and wag her tail back and forth. "We must celebrate!"

Virgyl and the wolves approach us, their own tails wagging happily. They lick Ryu, yipping and prancing around her. She pounces on them, trying to bite their tails.

Amalia and I sit on the forest floor, watching the animals play. I never thought I'd see the day when a Dyre Wolf pack adopted a Dragon, but she is one of them.

"I'll make the cave big enough for...for when she finishes growing. She will always be safe here; I'll make sure of it."

Amalia nods quietly, her face going slack. I feel her thoughts disappear elsewhere. She's been too tired, too withdrawn to wash her hair, so I've started washing it for her. It's still damp from when I washed it earlier, but as the strands dry, I can see it beginning to tangle.

"Come on, let's braid your hair. You might be a Wytch, but even Wytches need to brush their hair."

Amalia looks down at the ground, nudging a broken piece of bark with her foot. Her only response is to shrug.

Stay strong for her. She needs you.

"Come on," I grab her hand and gently pull her up. We walk back into the cave, sitting down in the area I carved out as a bedroom. The cave was already large, but I've created rooms and sections. Now there's privacy, should any of us want it.

I sit Amalia down on the pile of furs and pillows. She does so without argument, and I have to wonder if she's even here. Her body may next to me, but I can tell that her mind is far away. I grab a small, wide-toothed comb and begin brushing her long gray strands out.

Virgyl quietly pads in, carrying one of his newborn pups in his mouth, and drops it in Amalia's lap. The large black Dyre wolf curls around her, his yellow eyes wise and all-knowing.

We sit like that, the four of us. Ryu is eventually carried in by a large white wolf who deposits her alongside the pup in Amalia's lap. Ryu cuddles the wolf pup, immediately falling asleep.

The wolves follow suit, and I flick my hand, weaving a spell in my head to ignite the fire. Crackling sounds and vibrant orange glow illuminate the cave as the sky outside grows dark.

"There," I say as I finish combing the remaining tangles out of Amalia's hair. I quickly weave it into a three-strand braid, tying it off at the bottom with a small leather ribbon. "All done."

She nods, laying down on the pillows. The wolf pup and Ryu stay cuddled against her, while Virgyl adjusts to lay along her side.

"Thank you," Amalia says quietly.

I shake my head, placing my hand on her back. Leaning down, I lay beside her and begin rubbing slow, gentle circles along her spine.

"Don't thank me," I whisper. "I am happy to do it."

She nods but I can tell she doesn't believe it. I feel her sadness as the pillow beneath her face gets coated in tears.

I never stop rubbing her back.

I will *never* stop reminding her that I'm here. That's all I can do. That's all I *want* to do.

"I'm here, Ama." I press a kiss against her hair, inhaling her scent of bitter pomegranate. "I'm here."

She doesn't reply, but all of a sudden, a small, warm hand slides against mine. Amalia's fingers interlock with mine and she squeezes once.

The truth hits me like a falling tree to the chest.

Whatever she's feeling, this grief, this all-encompassing numb sadness; it doesn't mean she's not there. She just can't say much. As if the effort it takes to speak is far beyond her grasp.

She's still here.

And my words *help.* Even if she cannot say so.

Purpose fills me. Shining, glorious purpose.

Through the shadows, I look at the sight in front of me. At Amalia's sleeping figure, illuminated in firelight. At the Dyre Wolf pack that surrounds us, and the sleeping Dragon hatchling next to our clasped hands.

This is my family now.

This is what my family was always meant to be.

CHAPTER 37

NYALL

Year 500 PBM (9 months since the Arena Collapse)

Virgyl and I watch as Amalia attacks a tree with her swords. Ryu is off playing with the wolf pups under the watchful eye of Virgyl's mate, Syska.

I'm familiar with the Pack now, and they've grown more comfortable with me in return.

One of Virgyl's pups, a black wolf with white tipped fur, comes over to us and rubs against my legs.

"Hey, Bea."

Beatrice is her full name, but she's told me many times, she hates being called that.

Bea greets her father by licking his cheek.

"How is she?" Her voice is deep and scratchy.

"The pain will lessen...eventually." Virgyl replies, but we both hear the doubt in his voice.

"Or you could help her channel it," Bea suggests. *"Like last time."*

That catches my attention.

"Channel it?" I ask quietly.

Bea nods, her big orange eyes watching me. Her paws are nearly the size of my feet.

Virgyl lets out a deep sigh, looking up at the forest ceiling. *"Yes, perhaps you're right."*

"The Gray Wytch," I realize. "You...encouraged her to turn her grief into anger, using it to take out the Fae in the North."

Virgyl glances to the side, his yellow eyes all-knowing. When he looks at me, I get the feeling that Virgyl can see all of my secrets. As if he's reading my soul.

"Yes."

Virgyl looks at Bea, his eyes softening. *"You remember what happened last time, though. They had to leave, Bea. Now, we have something even more precious to protect. What if we're found?"*

Bea looks down, chagrined. *"I know. You're right."*

We fall silent, watching Amalia, who grunts and pants as she attacks the poor tree, wielding her blades with graceful, quick movements.

"Wait until Ryu is older," I say in their heads, my chest tight out of fear for both Amalia and the little Dragon. *"Wait until she can defend herself."*

For I am in love with them *both*.

Virgyl sighs. *"I did not wish this fate for her."*

"Yet it is her fate, nonetheless. She is the Right Hand," Bea reminds him with a whine. *"It is her destiny to get revenge. For her...for all of us."*

"Perhaps." Virgyl's voice is full of regret. *"But the Prince is correct. For now, Ryu is too young. It is best for Blue to stay here."*

I blink. "Blue?"

Bea sneezes and it sounds like a laugh.

"That is what we call Amalia," she says. *"Because of her eyes and her flames."*

Blue.

"It fits," I smile, feeling like I just learned an inside secret.

Ryu and the younger pups burst into the clearing, distracting Amalia from her relentless training. Sweat has turned her hair nearly black and stray strands plaster her forehead, having come loose from her braid.

Ryu screeches and pretends to tackle Amalia, who gives a small smile before falling to the ground, letting the little Dragon think she's won.

"Uh oh," Amalia says lightly. "Help!" she pretends to call, "I've been attacked by a Dragon!"

Ryu climbs onto Amalia's chest and licks her face. The pups join in and soon, giggles explode out of her.

"And some very naughty wolves!"

My eyes nearly close at the sound.

A glance to the side lets me know Virgyl is watching my reaction very closely. Not with judgement, but with unburned curiosity.

I shake it off. The Wolf can have his curiosity. That won't scare me away.

Nothing will.

Standing, I walk over to Amalia and hover over her as the wolf pups and Ryu torment her with cuddles.

"Need a rescue?"

Amalia laughs. "My *hero.*"

I hold out a hand and help her up, gently scooping Ryu into my arms at the same time.

The hatchling yawns, growing sleepy from the hours of roughhousing.

Then, the little red Dragon sneezes, unleashing a fireball at my face.

I expect pain but...nothing happens. Opening my eyes, I look down at her in confusion.

"Oops, sorry, Papa," Ryu squeaks.

I nearly drop her. With wide eyes, I look to the side, meeting Amalia's gaze which is full of shock.

We've told Ryu that we are not her parents. Neither of us want to diminish the Crimson Queen's memory. Ryu deserves to know about her.

I never thought this would be my life.

But it feels...right.

They feel right.

"Why didn't your flames hurt him, Ry?" Amalia asks gently, caressing Ryu's scales. "Do you know?"

"Yes! It's because I love you, silly."

We both fall silent.

"Dragons cannot hurt their family with their flames," Ryu explains. It's one of the longer sentences she's ever said and pride flows through me at her growing intelligence. *"I love you, so I can't hurt you."*

Goose bumps cover my arms, and my body grows warm as emotion chokes me up. Tears bead in the corners of my eyes and I blink them away.

"And I love you," I whisper, leaning down to press a kiss between her eyes. "So very much."

"As do I," Amalia whispers. "I will always love you, Ry. *Always.*"

"Love you, love you, Ama Mama," Ryu yawns and her eyes get heavy. The Dragon hatchling tucks her tail up and over her eyes, balling up in my arms as she drifts off to sleep.

I slowly look up, meeting Amalia's teary gaze. Her hand slides around my waist. It's rare that *she* initiates physical touch, but it makes moments like this mean that much more. My heart warms and the worries of the world lighten as I stand in the forest, cradled by my family.

It takes everything in my being not to turn to Amalia and tell her the truth. She's not ready for it yet, but I think she will be soon. Still, the thought of losing her, of saying anything that would push her further into the darkness...it terrifies me.

Amalia Asteroth's destiny is to be Morrigyn's hammer...but how do I tell her that my destiny is *her?*

CHAPTER 38
NYALL

Year 501 PBM (12 months since the Arena Collapse)

Ryu moans in her sleep as another growth spurt hits.

It's been like this every night for the past four weeks. The red hatchling is so big, I can no longer pick her up, even with my strength. It seems as if she nearly doubles in size nightly.

And it doesn't seem to be a comfortable process.

Seeing Ryu in pain has made Amalia and I restless. The growth spurts leave Ryu so tired, she's taken to napping in the cave during the day.

"I'm going to go pick some berries," Amalia calls.

"I'll come with you."

She nods and grabs a cotton bag. A few of the wolves join us as we disappear into the thick woods of the Ulster Wald.

The berry bushes are only a few minutes' walk away, but with winter quickly approaching, my cheeks soon turn numb.

We make it to the right spot and quickly begin picking berries off the branches, dropping them in the cotton bag. The light fabric blooms with deep purples and pinks.

Annoyed by the cold, I throw a quick weaving, a spell to create a shield full of heat.

This is one of the first weavings I ever learned. We had a terrible blizzard on my 25th year. My room was so cold, I could see every single breath.

The shield snaps into existence with a cracking sound and the air quickly turns balmy.

"That's quite handy," Amalia mentions with a happy sigh.

"It's saved me on many occasions."

There's a crunching sound and I look over to see Amalia toss a handful of berries into her mouth. The juice stains her lips a deep pink, drawing my attention.

"What?" she asks, bewildered.

I smirk. Reaching into the bag, I grab a handful of berries and do the same.

She snorts as my own lips turn deep pink.

"Oh shit," she chuckles. "I forgot how badly they stain."

"You lived out here on your own for so long; it's an easy thing to forget."

"Let me guess," she teases. "It's a good thing you're here now then, right?"

"You said it, not me." I wink at her. Her pale, freckled cheeks flush.

I don't know why I do it. But before I can think otherwise, I reach into the bag and grab more berries, stepping closer to Amalia.

She inhales sharply, her eyes wide as she looks up at me. I reach my hand up and run my thumb over the seam of her lips. She opens for me, and I nearly moan.

Instead, I slide a berry onto her tongue. She closes her lips around my finger, sucking lightly. Every nerve-ending in my body is set alight at her touch. I want to pick her up and haul her against the nearest tree, strip her naked, and lick her delicious body from head to toe. It's so bad, I'm trembling with need.

One of the wolves bumps into her leg and Amalia stumbles. We're both pulled out of the moment and quickly finish picking berries in quiet. The walk back to the cave is silent. In the distance, the suns have begun to set as the forest starts to grow dark.

The second we make it back, I get a fire going. A big one, suitable to keep the large cave plenty warm for us. Amalia slides a large cast iron pot onto a grate near the edge of the flames. Her veggie stew. Learning that Amalia Roth can cook—no, not just cook, but cook *extremely* well—was a damn shock. But one I'm immensely grateful for.

She sticks with stews, but every single time, she manages to take something that should be bland and make it full of flavor.

"It's the herbs," she told me the first time I asked her how she does it. "I just…understand what will work together."

The stew quickly heats, and I ladle us two bowls. We take a seat next to the fire and dig in. Soon, we're interrupted by Ryu who slowly walks past us.

"I'm going hunting," she says. *"I need food, and lots of it."*

I put the bowl down and walk over to her, placing my hand on the scales of her back. The spikes along her spine have gotten bigger—and sharper. I have to be careful where I place my hand, lest it get stabbed.

"The growth spurts—they're burning through my energy."

I nod. *"That makes sense, Ry. As you get bigger, you'll need more and more food."*

"I will accompany you. The pack could use a deer or two tonight." Virgyl approaches us, sitting on the hard stone floor next to me. Even seated, the Dyre Wolf is nearly as tall as I am.

"Be careful," Amalia says without turning.

Ryu snorts, *"Of course. We will be back soon. Come on, fuzz-butt."*

Virgyl bares his teeth, snapping at her foot. Not enough to hurt her, but it's his job as Alpha to teach the young. Ryu just rolls her eyes at him, *"I'm getting too big for that to work, you know."*

"No matter how big you get, you're still just a pup to me."

Ryu exhales. *"True."*

The two of them disappear into the night. Most of the pack follows, but Syska and Bea stay back to watch the younger wolves. Leaving Amalia and I completely alone.

Dinner is quiet. Both of us focus on eating, trying to ignore the searing tension in the air.

When Amalia is finished, I grab our now empty bowls and bring them into the kitchen area I created. It's simple but functional, which is all that matters.

"Wine?" I ask, grabbing a small wooden cask. Among the many things I've improved about the cave, a large pantry full of dried goods, dried fruits, cheeses, and wines is my favorite. Amalia had no way of storing food safely.

I keep it stocked with fresh herbs and root vegetables for her stews.

Amalia sighs, "Yeah, sure. Why not."

I uncork the bottle and pour some into two matching wooden mugs. I've been practicing some weavings to enhance the effectiveness of alcohol on Demis and Magyka. Arkaydians are similarly unaffected. Our metabolisms are too fast—we burn right through it.

I sit down next to Amalia and hand her a mug.

She tastes it and winces, "Fucking hell, that's strong."

I take a sip and it's an effort not to choke. It tastes awful. The room spins a bit, and I blink.

"Woah," Amalia gasps, leaning back in her chair. "What the hell did you do to that wine?"

Laughter explodes from me and a lightness settles around my shoulders. "We gotta pour that out. If I had a whole glass, I think it would kill me."

Amalia snorts, a smile breaking out on her face, "Three sips would kill me!"

"It was like drinking liquid fire. I thought I was going to choke on it."

"I almost spit it out, but I didn't want to hurt your feelings," she winks and my focus shifts.

I can't stop staring at her. She's so gorgeous. Her freckles are fading a bit, evidence of the days growing shorter and darker. This past summer they were so prominent. I want to kiss every single one.

"What?" Amalia laughs, touching her face. "Do I have something on my face?"

I shake my head. "No. I'm just looking at you."

"Why?" She smiles wryly.

God. She really doesn't know.

"Because," I pause, but the burn of alcohol has removed my walls. I can't stop now.

Clearing my throat, I begin again. "Because I care about you."

Because I care about you? Fuck me. That's terrible.

"I care about you too. Shockingly," Amalia admits, and I nearly fall off my seat.

But...

"That's not what I mean, Blue."

I don't know when we shifted but I'm suddenly terribly aware of how closely we're sitting. Her leg brushes against mine as Amalia adjusts. I grab her muscular calves and pull her closer, so that her legs are draped across my lap.

She's close enough to lean her head on my shoulder, but she just looks up at me, confusion and interest warring within her pale blue eyes.

"Let me try again," I take a deep breath. "I can't stop thinking about you."

Amalia's eyes widen.

"Every second of every day for the past year, you've been on my mind."

My eyes fall to her lips and the remainder of my patience implodes.

"Fuck it," I snarl, grabbing Amalia by the back of her head and tilting her head up as I lean down and press my lips against hers.

Amalia gasps and I swallow the sound, pulling back slightly. Her cheeks are a flushed pink and her pupils are blown as I pull away.

"I shouldn't have done that—"

Amalia dives towards me, smashing her lips against mine with an unleashed groan.

I meet her noise with one of my own as we fall back against the seat. Her scarred hands press against my chest as she grips the fabric of my shirt, yanking me closer. Her legs wrap around my waist as I use the tip of my tongue to coax her mouth open. She does, letting me in with a pleased sigh.

God. That *sound*.

Amalia Asteroth tastes like pomegranate honey.

I slide my hands into her soft gray hair, relishing this moment. How many times have I imagined this? Imagined the feeling of her plush lips on mine. Imagined her gasps of pleasure.

But I'm so fucking scared that if I screw this up, I'll lose her for good. So, my hands do not continue to wander, even though hers do. Every muscle in my body trembles as I strain to hold myself back.

This *has* to be on her terms. I promised Os that I would take care of her, and I meant it.

"Move your fucking hands," Amalia snarls.

"No," I whisper, sucking her bottom lip between mine. She lets out a moan and arches against me.

"Why not?"

"You need to say it. That you *want* this. That you want me."

Amalia groans in frustration. Her hands lift to my neck to pull me down closer.

Fucking hell. I could get *lost* in her.

"Ask me, Amalia," I croon. "Ask me to touch you. Ask me to make you feel good."

There's a noise in the distance that sounds suspiciously like a Dragon running into a tree.

But Amalia goes still. I pull back, unsure what's happening until I see her eyes. That glimmer of happiness and hope is gone. Sadness is all that's left.

Sadness and regret.

"I can't," she whispers, pulling away. I want to get down on my fucking knees and *beg* for her to let me explain.

To tell her why I understand.

"I hate this. I fucking hate this."

I don't know whether Amalia says that to herself, or me.

"Blue, I—"

"No, Nyall. Just stop. You don't get to call me that."

Logically, I understand that her sadness and fear is being channeled into anger. I'm old enough to know that; after all, I do the same. Have done the same for centuries.

Okay, Blue. I will play this part for you. Only for you.

"Does the fact that I've kept you safe for the past year mean fuck all to you?" The words taste like dust on my tongue. Lying to her *burns*. As if my insides are being charred by Hellfyre.

But it works. Too well.

I can see the moment she decides to push me away.

"I can keep myself safe," she looks away from me, examining the stone floor.

"I know you care about me, Amalia. What we've gone through...well, it changes you."

"I don't care about you." The words hit me like knives, but I can smell the lie in them.

"How long are you going to keep lying to yourself."

"Excuse me?" Amalia whirls, her eyes burning with anger. "Fuck you, Nyall. You want to talk about lying to yourself? What's the rebel leader doing hiding out in a cave with a wanted fugitive and some wolves? What kind of leader abandons his people?"

I knew it was coming. But goddamnit, that hurts. Because I know it's true.

I have known the whole time.

Amalia just doesn't realize I will always choose her. Over any*thing* and every*one.*

"You're right," I say coldly, looking to the side. The coldness is real, not at her but at the reality of our situation.

I could stay here forever, and I would—but I shouldn't.

"I know," is all she says, before retreating into the bedroom.

Bracing my arms on my legs, I slide my head into my hands, wishing desperately I could erase the past few minutes.

"She's not ready," Virgyl says in my mind. I didn't hear him approach but a single glance to my right confirms the giant black Dyre Wolf is now seated by the fire, staring at me with his big yellow eyes.

"Their memories are too fresh in her mind and heart," he says to me. *"Amalia allows the world to assume she does not feel, but the truth is, my cub feels so strongly it destroys her."*

I suspected the same.

"Anger is better than her suffocating from the ghosts of her past."

"I know," I admit to him.

"Then you are leaving."

I meet his gaze and nod, sadly. *"Yes. Tomorrow morning."*

"Where will you go?"

"The Rebel camp down South."

Virgyl watches me carefully. *"It is no longer in the South though, is it Prince?"*

How the *fuck* did the wolf figure that out?

"That is an answer for another time. I did not say anything because I approve. It's best for you to stay close."

I blink, so shocked I think I forget to breathe.

"Ryu will be sad, but she will understand," Virgyl says finally. *"Will you tell her the truth?"*

I sigh and smile sadly, *"Yes. I will. Although I think she already knows."*

I glance behind me and watch as the red Dragon quietly walks into the room. For something so large, she's light on her feet.

Ryu nuzzles me, licking my cheek. *"I do not want you to go, but I know why you must."*

Reaching a hand up, I caress her scales. *"I will always be here if you need me. All you need to do is reach out with your magyk. I will hear you."*

"I know, Papa," Ryu says quietly. *"Old fuzz-butt and I will take care of Ama. We will help her work through this."*

I nod. *"I will send a hawk with letters for her once a month, checking in."*

"She won't answer," Virgyl says sadly.

"I don't care. I refuse to let her think I've forgotten about her."

"You are a good male, Prince Drayven." Virgyl bows lightly and it's like the world stops for a moment. There's a weight to the air within his movements. *"Ready your people and raise your army. We will need it for what's ahead."*

I fear he's right.

I do not sleep, even when the pack falls silent. They crowd around me, pressing near. I don't know when the pack accepted me, but I am grateful for their friendship. This is not the life I thought I would have, but I would take this fucking cave over Castael Laryn any day. I just wish Amalia could see that I love it here. That I love her.

"She will," Ryu whispers at my back. I'm leaning against her warm neck. Glancing to the left, I meet her eyes. *"She will see it eventually. When the time is right, we will show her, and I will help."*

I caress the scales of her cheek. "I know."

Eventually, they fall asleep, while I stay wide awake, thinking about the Gray Wytch of the Ulster Wald—the Wytch who has stolen my heart.

CHAPTER 39
VESIMYR

Dyana has been asleep for over a year.

The redhead Demis keeps asking when Dyana will wake up, but I do not have an answer.

What I have done has never been done before.

So I will sit and I will wait; as long as it takes. Dyana Arkos will wake up some day, but I do not know when that day is. I do know that when the day finally comes, she's going to change the world.

Mirielle sighs in her chair by Dyana's bed. I'm on the roof, listening in, though I can see the room in my mind's eye.

I can see everything related to Dyana now. We are connected. We share *blood*. She is my child as much as she is my charge.

The redhead loves her, my Dyana.

It is plain to see.

Whether or not Dyana loves the redhead...we will find out. The longer Dyana is asleep, the more our situation here becomes dire.

Elysium is not the paradise I remember. Ignautius, the Sene Skal, is a tyrant who feeds on the pithy prayers of his worshippers.

Ignautius and his followers are going to be a problem; but not yet.

Dyana will wake up to a world in chaos.

A small finch lands on my head.

"Have message?" it chirps in my mind.

"Yes, I do," but...the journey is long. *"Share the burden with others in your flock. The message is short, but I need to find someone in Ur Daoine."*

I relay the message after the finch agrees. It flies off, heading for its flock. Together, they will share the message and fly it across the Midheym Sea.

The world is changing fast. Preparations must be made for what's to come.

I just hope Dyana is ready. Her fate was sealed the moment my blood entered her system and the magyk I kept hidden for so long finally unleashed. Like a seed, it's rooting within her soul.

Only time will tell if she withers or blooms.

CHAPTER 40
MIRIELLE

"Please wake up," I whisper.

Dyana does not respond.

Her body is so still, I sometimes wonder if she is even alive.

Then I'll see her chest rise. Every time, it's a weight off my shoulders.

She's not dead. She's going to wake up.

I repeat the words over and over, praying to Lir that they're true.

"Get some rest," a deep voice says in my head. I glance to my right to see Vesimyr's huge head leaning into the window. He crawls down from the roof, gracefully maneuvering his large body halfway into the room.

It used to scare me when he did that, bursting into my thoughts with no prior warning. Now, I expect it.

"I am not tired," I tell him.

"It was not a request. Get some rest. Focus on your new role." Vesimyr stares at me, his bright green eyes glowing. A nasty scar bisects his right eye, making him look all the more terrifying.

I look away and reach over to clasp Dyana's hand. Mine are stained with oil and smudges of coal. Blisters and callouses cover my fingers, a side effect of my new role here.

I've taken up work at the mortal forge, apprenticing under the blacksmith there. Forsaken crumbled into the Earth, so I will build one anew.

"Will she ever wake?" I ask the great silver Dragon.

It's the same question I ask every day, and every day, he gives the same answer.

"Someday."

That's not good enough, though. Someday could be in a hundred years. That's but a blink of an eye in the lifespan of a Dragon. We don't have a hundred years. We don't even have five years.

I need Dyana to wake up, because I need her help. We have to get out of here, before it's too late.

"Wake up," I whisper. "We need you. *I* need you. You just have to open your eyes."

Dyana's body remains still.

Weary, I stand and leave the room. The silver Dragon makes a large thumping noise as he moves fully into the room. I glance back, watching as he curls around Dyana's bed.

CHAPTER 41
VIRGYL

"Will you tell her?" Syska asks.

Bea and the others gather round. Amalia and Ryu are already asleep; the former exhausted from crying all day.

Nyall left this morning.

Amalia leans on the big red Dragon, who is curled around her for protection.

"Not yet," I sigh. *"It's not the right time."*

Syska lets out a low whine and nuzzles into me. *"Will there ever be a right time?"*

"Yes. I can feel it fast approaching. Soon, she will need to know the truth. They all will. He is becoming too big of a problem to avoid."

I think back to the day Amalia and her Prince showed up. I felt it; the ripple that shook the world. A few days later, another, different ripple hit me. One that I recognized.

A bird chirps incessantly overhead, interrupting my thoughts. Something about its coloring stands out. It's white and gray, with a red patch on its chest and head.

It's some kind of finch, but not one I've ever seen before.

Others with similar coloring follow it.

I connect with the small creature.

"Message," it says in a high-pitched voice. *"Have message."*

"What is the message?"

"It's time," the creature responds. "The bones have been buried."

I thank the bird and it flies away, the others in its flock following suit. The words ring in my head.

Yes, the truth will be revealed all too soon.

Syska is quiet for a moment. *"I am scared, Virgyl. I am scared for what will happen when that day comes."*

"Do not be afraid, my love." I lay down and she does the same. We curl up together, breathing in each other's scent.

My mate. My everything.

"Nothing will happen to the Ulster Wald, or any who dwell within it. On this, I swear."

"That's what I'm afraid of," she whispers. *"What you'll do to keep that promise. I don't want to lose you—"*

"You will never lose me, Sys. Never."

She nods but I feel her doubt. Eventually, she falls asleep like the others, until it's just me still awake. I can feel their bright minds drifting off in peace.

I don't know how to tell her that I'm afraid too.

CHAPTER 42
OS

When they hauled my broken body out of the Arena, I wasn't thankful.

I wanted them to let me die, but the Archmage forced my shattered body to heal.

My legs were too destroyed. They had to cut them off and grow them back. I welcomed the drugs. Welcomed the detachment, because I knew, even then, that the second I was healed, the interrogations would begin.

The Archmage thinks I can be broken.

Little does he know; I've been broken this entire time. Carve me away piece by piece until there's nothing left; it will make no difference.

No amount of torture will make me tell them about my familiar.

"Give me something, Os. Please. Tell me where she is."

I spit in her face, and she flinches.

"I'm trying to be nice, Os, but the more shit like this you pull, the more my patience wanes," Ireyna slams her palm down on the metal table. "I'm trying to help you get out of here. Accept Him into your heart. He will forgive you! Just tell me what you know about Amalia Asteroth."

Amalia.

Her name settles into my skin, sinking all the way into my blood and my bones.

Amalia.

She's alive—and not here, thank fuck.

But she's alive.

AMALIA!

My familiar is alive, and they want her.

Over my dead body.

I yank the metal cuffs so hard, they break off the table they were previously attached to. Leaping over the table, I charge at Ireyna with a roar.

She scrambles out of the room, slamming the door in my face.

So, I take it down.

The skin falls off of my knuckles as I pummel the metal door over and over again. I can hear the screams of the guards outside.

Good; let them *scream.*

I don't care how long it takes, but when I get out of here, I'm going to *burn them to ash.*

Eventually, guards armed with metal prods storm the room.

I kill three of them before the crowd is able to subdue me.

"Restrain him." I hear Ireyna's voice in the distance.

"Torture me all you like. I'll never tell you where she is, you fucking cunt."

"Pity. Regrowing your legs for a second time will be...arduous." Something hits me in the face and the world fades to black

When I wake, all I know is blood and pain.

THE END
IS BEGINNING

xoxo, EG

THE DRAGON QUEEN SERIES CONTINUES...

AMALIA ROTH IS DEAD. She died alongside the Crimson Queen in the arena two years ago. Donning her Gray Wytch persona, Amalia and the Dragon Ryu have spent the past year hunting down the Fae who wronged her.

Across the Midheym Sea on the isle of Elysium, Dyana grapples with her new-found magyk under the guidance of the ancient dragon, Vesimyr. She quickly learns that Elysium isn't paradise—it's a prison. Trapped under the claws of the Dragon Regent, she cannot leave. But Dyana knows Amalia is alive and will stop at nothing to get back to her sister—even if it means taking on the Regent alone.

The rebel Mirielle has lost everything. Her life's goal was to take down the High Council, but doing so only made things worse. Lost and alone, Mirielle begins plotting a way back home, regardless of the risks.

With the High Council gone, the Archmage has risen. Storms shake the continent as the situation grows more dangerous by the day. Ur Daoine lies on the brink of civil war. In secret, the heretic Prince Nyall Drayven leads the growing rebellion. After Nyall convinces Amalia to join him at the front, a divide within the rebel factions, and his carefully built control begins to crumble.

When one of the rebels' carefully planned missions goes wrong, a familiar face steals Ryu and reveals a truth that will change everything; someone from Amalia's past is alive.

FROM ASHES AND PAIN, AMALIA ASTEROTH HAS RISEN.

THE DEFIANT AND THE DAMNED

The Dragon Queen: Book 2

Coming February 25, 2025

Scan the QR Code below to Pre-Order.

GLOSSARY

Abhaynn Gheal: A large river just south of Castael Laryn, the capital city of Ur Daoine.

ABM: Ante Bellum Magni, which means Before Great War. The years prior to the Fae taking control of the Kingdom.

Achan Drayven: High Councilor and leader of all Fae. Age is unknown. Was present when the Fae arrived 600 years ago.

A gahrá: Means "my beloved" in the language of the Dragons. There is no true translation because Dragons have three vocal cords, and their words are made up of sounds Os cannot make in human form.

Ahavah: Means "my heart" in the language of Amalia's father and his kin.

Amalia Roth: A woman who seems to be in her late 20s. Amalia lives in Twyn Fells, a town in the far north of Ur Daoine, where she passes for a human. Amalia hides her true identity, but she is the last living Arkaydian, an ancient breed of magical being with powers that relate to living things and nature.

The Annag: A small forest to the West of Castael Laryn.

Archidna: A spider-like monster with sharp pincers and eight legs. They vary in size from a small pony to a full-size horse.

The Archmage: The position of High Councilor Achan Drayven's right hand. Filled by a powerful Fae.

Arkaydia: An ancient Magykal kingdom that has since disappeared.

Beastkyn: Animals with the ability to turn into people. Not shifters, but true animals that just change shape. Very rare.

The Black Citadel: The High Council's fortress, in the center of Castael Laryn.

Castael Laryn: The capital city of Ur Daoine and seat of power of the Imperial Fae.

Dark Magyk: A forgotten, evil type of magyk practice first created by the elves thousands of years ago. The reason the elves destroyed their homeland and went extinct. Dark magyk users should be avoided at all costs.

Demis: The offspring of a human or other Magyka breeding with a Fae. Demis simply means part Fae.

Dragons: Four and two-legged creatures widely regarded to be Gods. They're made of magyk. Dragons first originated in their homeland, Elysium, which lies to the far west, across the Midheym Sea.

Dragonfear: A biological phenomenon that occurs in lower beings such as humans, Demis, and Magyka when they lay eyes upon a Dragon. The more magyk a being possesses, the easier it is to shrug Dragonfear off. Dragonfear causes heart palpitations, high blood pressure, anxiety, and panic, as it instigates a fight or flight response.

Dragonguard: The personal Dragon Riders of the High Council. The Dragonguard is made up of a dozen or so tamed, lab-bred Dragons that have been domesticated. Only Imperial Fae have been able to ride Dragons, as the rest were eaten upon attempt. The Dragonguard patrols the borders and carries out assignments from the High Council, including the rounding up of Gauntlet candidates.

Dyana Arkos: A human orphan, adopted sister of Amalia Roth. 24 years old and is a professional dancer at the Birdcage.

The Dragon Pit: The caverns that house the Dragons. Formerly a temple to the Morrigyn, for 500 years it's been a stable for Dragons.

The Eastlands: The Eastern district of Ur Daoine. Known for being a big fruit and vegetable producer in the country.

Eahmond: A northland town, the closest down to Twyn Fells.

Elves: An extinct group of highly Magykal beings who wielded dark magyk, a type of magyk that can suck the life out of anything living. There are rumors of some elves that are still alive, but the ages of the elves have centuries passed.

Elysium: The legendary kingdom of the Dragons. Thought to be a myth. Elysium is surrounded by a giant wall of clouds that hide the most complex, advanced ward that has ever been woven. This ward keeps everyone that isn't a Dragon out. Only a Dragon can grant passage to a lower being, but once you enter, the wards will never let you out.

Fae: A powerful race of supernaturals who appeared within a portal 600 years ago to take control of Arkaydia. After 100 years of war, they emerged victorious and now rule. Fae possesses heightened strength and hearing, and the royals hold magyk.

The Father: A version of Sol Constantus. A side sect of Sol Constantus believers pray to The Father. They believe that Sol Constantus and The Father are separate but equal.

The Fray: A monthly tournament where the top fighters in the kingdom fight each other and dragons, for the entertainment of the Fae.

The Gauntlet: A tournament to the death held every 25 years where 30 candidates, two humans from every town in the Kingdom, compete for a prize and the right to live.

The Gray Wytch: A legendary figure used to scare children into behaving. The Gray Wytch is thought to be dead, now, but she lived deep within the Ulster Wald with her pack of wolves, hunting down bad Fae and misbehaving children.

The High Council: The Imperial Fae rulers who formerly ruled Ur Daoine, made up of four councilors and a High Councilor. Highly skilled magyk users. The High Council are now deceased.

Humans: The bottom species of Ur Daoine, a race with no special abilities

Mrs. Hunton: Innkeeper and bar owner where Amalia rents her room. Wife to Mr. Hunton, owner of Taran the horse. Amalia gets a discounted rental rate in exchange for caring for and riding Taran at the stables.

The Infinium Sands: A large desert to the southwest of Ur Daoine.

Ireyna: Unknown species. Gauntlet trainer.

Kydis: The Crimson Queen, a great red dragon and the rightful ruler of Elysium. Ancient and very powerful.

Lir: The Arkaydian God of the Sea. Believers of Lir lived in the area that is now called the Eastlands. Few pray to Lir openly.

Macha: One of the two swords of Morrigyn, gifted to Arkaydia over two thousand years ago and hidden deep in the caves, only to be found by Remus Ostia five centuries ago. The pair to Neiman.

Magyka: Non-Fae Magykal beings including shifters and vampires.

The Midheym Sea: The sea to the west of Ur Daoine.

Mirielle Zenyth: Unknown species. The candidate is from Sud Azul in the Eastlands. Her partner ran away the first day, so she has no partner.

The Morrigyn: One form of the Mother. The Arkaydian Goddess of War and Wisdom. Formerly had the world's largest temple devoted to Her. Few pray to her anymore.

The Mother: One form of the Morrigyn. The Arkaydian Goddess of Creation. She has two sides to represent the duality of being. For all light, there is dark. The Mother is the light, the Morrigyn is the dark.

Neiman: One of the two swords of Morrigyn, gifted to Arkaydia over two thousand years ago and hidden deep in the caves, only to be found by Remus Ostia five centuries ago. The pair to Macha.

Nyall Drayven: Crown Prince of Ur Daoine.

The Northlands: The Northern Territory of Ur Daoine. The biggest land wise but the least populated due to the Ulster Wald. Also called the "North."

Oryx: A rare breed of warhorse with a swirling black horn, eyes like rubies, and sharp fangs for teeth. Oryx are 25% bigger than a normal warhorse and have twice the speed and endurance. Oryx hasn't been seen in the Infinium Sands, their hibernation grounds, for centuries.

Pass of Brón Mór: A narrow and dangerous pass between the mountains of the Ulster Wald.

PBM: Post Bellum Magni, which means After Great War. The years following the Fae taking control of the Kingdom.

Puggō: A slur for humans.

Remus Ostia: Dragon Beastkyn. Head trainer of the Gauntlet. Extremely dangerous and powerful, approach with caution.

Shifters: People with the ability to turn into animals.

Siphon: A higher level magyk user with the ability to drain the lifeforce from any living being as well as the earth itself and transfer it to themselves or to another source. They can literally siphon and move magyk. Siphons are almost always of Elvish descent.

The Southlands: The Southern district of Ur Daoine, which includes the Infinium Sands.

Sol Constantus: The national religion of Ur Daoine, of which they pray to the Father, Constanus. It wasn't illegal to pray to one of the other Gods but only allowed in private.

Sud Azyl: A port town in the Eastlands, and a large supplier of food for Ur Daoine.

Taran: Originally the horse belonging to Mrs. Hutton's husband, Taran has been cared for by Amalia for years and now belongs to her. Taran is a large white horse with gray dapples and a black mane and tail.

Twyn Fells: The Northernmost town in Ur Daoine.

The Ulster Wald: A sprawling forest that takes up most of the Northern territory.

Ur Daoine: A large country ruled by the Fae. Ur Daoine is divided into four territories; The North (composed mainly of the massive Ulster Wald forest), The Westlands, The Southlands (with the Infinium Sands), and the Eastlands.

The Westlands: The smallest territory of Ur Daoine to the West of the Abhaynn Gheal and South of the Ulster Wald.

Weaving: A term used by some to describe magyk castings. Weavers use a combination of incantations and hand movement to pull visible magyk from the air. It's one of the few types of magyks that are always visible, outside of shifters.

Wytch: Humans, fabled to have Fae-like powers. No proof of a Wytch has ever been found.

THANK YOU

Where do I even begin? First and foremost, I want to thank the animals who have saved my lifetime and time again. When the depression makes everything seem hopeless, and when my anxiety makes me too scared to move, the love of animals always brings me back into the light. **Boomer, Luca, Flynn, Beau, Blue, Xena, Stanley, Tosh, Artemis, Sophie, Jinx, Evie, Carmen, Lady...** I could go on. **Frankie,** thank you for being my best friend, even if it ended up that I'm your Emotional Support Human instead of you being my Emotional Support Animal. I never thought I could love something as much as I love you. Thank you for always licking up my tears and loving me more than anything on this planet.

The animal industry is incredibly cruel. Everything in this book is inspired by real situations that happen to animals in this world every single fucking day. I hope this book sheds some light on the ways animals are suffering; and how, even in the face of cruelty, they have so much love to give us.

Secondly, but not least, thank you to my parents. **Mom and Dad,** thank you for always supporting me, even when I announce I'm going to completely change careers and give writing a real chance. Thank you for keeping me afloat and giving me a support system I can rely on, even when I feel lost and alone.

To the entire **Schaeffel Clan, Wolski Clan, and Garrett Clan,** thank you for making me feel like I'm not alone in this world. Moving back to the Midwest and being able to see you all on a regular basis is such a joy.

To my friends. **Tiffany, Lyss, Corrine, Becky + DJ, Reina, Marilu, Lindsay, Reina, Beth, Rachel, Alexa, Gabi, & Esther**– I love you all so much and I'm so thankful to have you in my life. Distance and time will never push us apart.

To my writing group, the **Trash Bandits.** Thank you for encouraging me to sprint even on the days when I don't feel like it. **CK Beggan, Reina, Trent, Lindsay, David, and Marilu Moser.** It's an honor to write alongside you all and to call you, my friends.

To my amazing editor **YarnWyvern**; infinite thanks and gratitude for your friendship, mentorship, and your keen eye. You improved this story so much, and I am so thankful.

To my PA **Molly.** Thank you for being my official chaperone and keeping me on track. But thank you most of all for being my friend. You're stuck with me forever now.

To my **Alpha and Beta readers.** Your feedback made this book what it is. Thank you for always answering my 2:00 a.m. insane questions with no context. Thank you for the honesty and thoughtfulness behind every opinion and answer. I am beyond grateful for all of you.

To my **Kickstarter backers.** You made me believe in myself, which is no easy feat. Thank you for taking a chance on me and showing me that my ideas are worthy. I'm still in shock at your generosity and am endlessly grateful. All of you have a permanent place at my table.

To the **University of Nevada, Reno, and the College of Liberal Arts.** The History, Philosophy, and English classes that I took molded me into the person I am today. Liberal Arts degrees are incredible, and I hope to see more funding for Liberal Arts colleges in the future. Thank you for fueling my desire to learn and how to ask the right questions. To the Professors and teachers who molded me, I owe my success to you. Thank you for your patience with my endless questions.

<u>**REPUBLICA HELVETORUM**</u>

gothic monster romance
Here There Be Monsters
Here There Be Witches – *coming 2026*
There Are Monsters Beneath – *coming 2026/2027*

<u>**THE DRAGON QUEEN**</u>

dark epic fantasy
The Forgotten and The Feared
The Broken and The Brave
The Defiant and The Damned
TDQ3 – *coming 2026*

<u>**THE HOME FOR WAYWARD CREATURES**</u>

paranormal romantic sci-fi
Vol. 1
Vol. 2 – coming 2027

<u>**SHORT STORIES & SERIALS**</u>
Rescue Me – *contemporary fiction*
FERN – *sci-fi horrormance*
DARKMOOR – *gothic why-choose romance*

EC Garrett is an Alaskan transplant now living in Kansas City, MO who writes fantasy/sci-fi speculative fiction. She received her Bachelor's Degree in English Literature with a focus in Early Modern and Medieval Literature and a minor in Medieval History from the University of Nevada, Reno in 2016. EC hopes to get her Masters in English Literature as well. In her spare time, she's either reading or watching the latest fantasy releases, riding horses at the barn, spending time with her family, or playing with her very cute but extremely ornery dachshund mix, Frankie.

She dreams of becoming a dragon rider.

Follow ECG on social media to get all the latest updates.

www.authorecgarrett.com

Instagram: @authorecgarrett

Tiktok: @author.ecgarrett

Threads: @authorecgarrett

Facebook: @authorecgarrett

Join ECG's exclusive reader membership, **The Scale Society Community** for a bonus scenes, serial stories, access to ECG's private reader Discord, and so much more.

Scan or click to join today! Trust me, you don't want to miss this.

Midnight Pages

indie publishing house + bookish candles
handmade in kansas city, mo

www.ingramcontent.com/pod-product-compliance
Lightning Source LLC
Chambersburg PA
CBHW070415310726
48977CB00003B/694